A novel by
DAVID IRONS

Based on the screenplay by
ROBERT McGINLEY

Encyclopocalypse Publications
www.encyclopocalypse.com

First Edition, 2025
ISBN: 978-1-966037-19-4

Cover artwork elements used with permission from Boom! Cult
Layout and design by Sean Duregger
Interior formatting by Mark Alan Miller and Sean Duregger
Edited by Mike Watt

Passages from *The Tragedy of Orpheus and Eurydice*, Ovid,
Metamorphoses Book 10:1-86; 11:1-84, translated by
Brookes More (Boston: Cornhill Publishing Co., 1922).

Foreword

My journey with *Shredder Orpheus* began as a happy accident. When a friend on the Internet mentioned an 80's movie with Orpheus as a rock star with a headband that they couldn't remember the name of, I took to searching. While it wasn't the movie my friend was thinking of (the French film *Parking* by Jacques Demy), I found *Shredder Orpheus* in the process and have never looked back since. However you have happened to find this book, whether recommended or by chance, I hope *Shredder Orpheus* stays with you as it has me.

If you're unaware of the basics of the myth behind the story, here's a quick rundown: The musician and poet Orpheus, said to be one of the greatest in the world, married the lovely nymph Eurydice. Their happiness was short-lived, however, as Eurydice was bitten by a snake and died, casting her soul to Hades, the Greek Underworld. Orpheus became determined to rescue his wife and descended to the Underworld with the power of his music overcoming all obstacles. His lyre playing was so persuasive it even got Hades and Persephone, the king and queen of the dead, to agree to give Eurydice back—on a condition: He must not look back until they'd reached the surface to-gether. Depending on which version you read there's several reasons why Orpheus ultimately turned around too soon, but turn he did, losing Eurydice once more.

On paper, the film's premise is decidedly weird as it updates the myth of Orpheus and Eurydice to play out in a post-apocalyptic world filled with soul-sucking TV broadcasts, where Hades and Persephone's Euthanasia Broadcast Network rules with an iron first and distracts the masses while slowly killing them. When Eurydice is killed at her own wedding so the network can acquire her dancing talents, Orpheus speeds to the rescue with a mystical Lyre-Axe Guitar supposedly made by Jimi Hendrix. A Greek chorus of skateboarders watches the tale unfold from the outside, and Orpheus's mythological journey isn't the end of things—not to spoil too much for those who haven't seen it, but he eventually gets a second chance to save the woman he loves, and it in-volves shredding on a magic skateboard from the depths of Hades itself.

One element that makes the film work is how sin-cere it is about the world that it creates and the char-acters live in. There's enough exposition to build the world and provide explanations, but there's more than enough room for the viewer to become curious about how and why things work. The more fantastic elements are accepted by the characters as natural de-spite the strangeness, not questioned or seen as unbe-lievable—and of the few moments that *are*, they're given enough pathos and time for the reality of the situations to sink in, and are treated as normal there-after. The viewer accepts any weirdness as just part of the world they live in, just like real life.

Another element that enhances the film is the

characters themselves, who are all memorable in their own ways. Orpheus's love for Eurydice is sincere and colors nearly everything he does, while Eurydice loves him back just as much but isn't afraid to tease him over his loud rock music. Orpheus's manager Linus starts as a funny, camp character before revealing his own hidden anger and frustration in the second half of the film. Hades, the ruler of the underworld, seems married to the job as well as his wife Persephone, who takes an interest in Orpheus alongside the network's drive to claim Eurydice. The Greek chorus of skaters are clearly defined as well, with Axel as a tough-talking war veteran who's wise even in (especially in) anger, Razoreus as an edgy, emotional young boy who sees Orpheus as an older brother, and Scratch as an androgyne health food freak who skates with the best of them, but bears a quiet jealousy of Eurydice and Orpheus's interest in her—and guilt when it all goes wrong. An oracle only appears in one scene, but her tarot reading provides important clues for the finale and her way of giving advice is all tough love.

The final element that makes the film work, and arguably the most important, is the emotion behind everything. Losing Eurydice completely wrecks Orpheus mentally and physically to the point of being deeply depressed, but the viewer might not notice at first because he's out skating with friends and going to his concerts. But when the lights are down and he's home alone, it's clear that Eurydice was everything to him, and activities he used to love alongside her now mean nothing to him. Eurydice doesn't have it much better as she's forced to dance for the network alongside Hades himself, her sad eyes both accusing and apologetic. With Linus trying to tell him to move on to no avail, and Hades and Persephone displeased with Eurydice's performance, it's both a relief and an ominous warning when Orpheus does get a second chance to save Eurydice.

This novelization captures all of what makes the film work and more (for best results you can listen to the soundtrack LP whilst reading). David Irons has included some never-before publicized scenes from an early draft script to add flavor, and has adapted the uncut script from the recent Blu-Ray release, which contains extended scenes not seen on VHS or DVD before—and adds additional drama, humor, and heart to what's already there. The film is an unknown gem that deserves to be seen by a wider audience, and whether you're a returning fan coming to check out the novel, or someone who's never heard of *Shredder Orpheus* before now, I hope it lives up to your expectations.

As Hades and Persephone Hecata would say: *Praise the Ray...*

But as Orpheus and Eurydice Hellenbach would say: **Screw that!**

Amy Rose
Mythologist and Shredder Orpheus Historian

Introduction

Robert McGinley

Shredder Orpheus was born in 1987 on late summer nights when I joined a pack of ramp shredding skate boarders infiltrating downtown Seattle parking garages. We snuck into elevators traveling 8-12 stories high and flew down the garage ramps in an adrenalized, wipe out-death defying ecstasy until the police or security guards chased us out.

As a mythology student, Z-Boys/Bones Brigade Video fan and indie punk filmmaker, I saw parallels between skating into the bowels of a parking garage was similar to Orpheus going to hell into the underworld of Hades. In the pantheon of Greek Mythology heroes, the Orpheus journey celebrates the artist-musician as the only mortal to ever journey to the world of the dead and survive. His journey to seek his love, Eurydice, in the underworld and return presents a potent boon for humanity that demonstrates that the emotional power of love is stronger than death. Consequently, this metaphysical boon from Orpheus activated a personal "call" for me to embark on my own artist-filmmaking journey to the underworld and, in retrospect, was subconsciously triggered by the loss of a girlfriend in a traffic accident.

In the end, combining the myth of Orpheus, the virtuosic musical icon, with skateboarding culture and the soul sucking medium of commercial broadcast TV seemed like a great way to update and recreate the oldest love story in Western Civilization and exercise my passionate belief that love is the life force antidote to death.

David Irons, in adapting the film and script into novel form, has breathed new life into the *Shredder Orpheus* mythos. His nuanced storytelling expands on film's foundations, delivering an electrifying fusion of love, death and rock 'n roll.

I hope this novel and the film inspires you to shred through life's challenges, embracing the power of love and creativity along the way. SHRED ON!

Robert McGinley
Writer and Director of *Shredder Orpheus*

In loving memory of Carlo Scandiuzzi.

L to R: Gian Carlo Scandiuzzi (Hades, King of the Underworld), Jackson Cooper (American Genre Film Archive), Robert McGinley (Orpheus; Writer / Director), Vera McCaughan (Persophone, Queen of the Underworld)

The television set switched on automatically, and from the darkness bloomed light. EBN – the Euthanasia Broadcast Network – controlled all the screens, but this message was for a specific audience, sent out into the ether to hunt its prey.

The message cryptic, scrolling left to right in bright blue letters, like the Stock Exchange would, before the war. An important Ovideo:

> "O deities of this dark world beneath the
>   earth!
> this shadowy underworld, to which
> all mortals must descend!"

The message delivered, the screen went dead once more, and darkness overtook the light.

The worn bearings in Axel's wheels rumbled along concrete as grey as TV static. His beaten-up skateboard wobbled from side to side as he skidded to a stop. He didn't use his deck like all the others; he had to sit on the damn thing, legs stretched out, as he pounded the ground with hands shrouded by thick welding gloves to propel himself forward. Not that calloused hands mattered. Not that anything fucking mattered. Who the fuck was he kidding? It was more like a wheelchair than a skateboard.

On the outside, Axel looked like a successful mutation of the times. A twisted, bespectacled face framed by a worn leather aviator cap. His clothes were sooty and threadbare. He was a veteran of the Contra Drug Wars. 101st Air Cavalry. Three years in Central American jungles left Axel without the use of his hips and a nervous system ripped to shreds. All he had was his deck and the clothes on his back.

Most of his senses might be shattered, but he felt something watching him now. Axel jerked to his right and saw the huge Euthanasia Broadcast Network satellite dish. It was on top of the monolithic EBN glass building, and it beamed down at him like a giant eye.

Axel tore his gloves off as he stared back into the EBN dish, his body twitching in repulsion.

That dish was constantly spewing cathode cancer rays into the sky, beaming down to screens and monitors with scan lines as thick as bars.

If only he had some of his gear from the war. A high-powered shell would turn the dish to dust. That would teach those EBN fucks.

Axel tried to calm his nerves, reached inside his shirt pocket, pulled out a warm Cherry Coke, popped the top, and chugged the syrupy brown liquid.

He stared up at the EBN tower and the dull-eyed dish on top. EBN; the whole station was something right out of Hell. No, Hell was supposed to be warm. The EBN tower was cold — dead cold and looked like a propped-up corpse in a glass coffin.

TV could have been a window to the imagination.

TV had the potential to reach the masses with a message.

EBN had cheapened it to soul-sucking banality.

"Some friend you turned out to be," Axel growled at the dish.

He remembered better times than these. He remembered the days when people started getting addicted to the video dross beamed by EBN. He tried to warn them. Nobody listened. No one ever listened. Screaming at the dish didn't change anything, but it helped him deal with the anger.

Axel chugged more of the warm brown liquid, staring at the dish as it stared at him. It was all old advertising bullshit.

EBN: America's real choice.
Red, White, and You.
Catch the Wave.

They were all catching the wave, all right. Beamed from that fucking dish straight into their smooth brains.

EBN had poisoned the world with recreational rays, and everyone had laid back and taken it. He should have fought back, tried to make a difference, and stopped the morons from reaching out to touch the tube.

"You didn't give me a chance!" Axel yelled, eyeing the soulless dish for a reply. "You let the whole damn thing slide down the toilet. Now what you got? *Shit!*"

Fucking tower.

Fucking dish.

Fucking EBN.

They were the ones responsible for this burnt-out, smoldering butt of a world.

"You don't even know what's going on, do ya?" Axel cried. "What do you think I got? *Not shit!*"

He poured the Cherry Coke over the concrete, turning it a sludgy brown. *Matches the souls of the fucks in that fucking building*, Axel thought, and then slammed the empty can to the ground.

"It's all piss anyway," he growled. Then, he awkwardly pulled his welding gloves on and pushed himself off, riding back into the Grey Zone.

2

Axel rolled into the Marginal Way Village Housing Project — the Grey Zone. Surviving the war was one thing. Surviving this place was another. The city's answer to low-income housing was five acres of neon spray-painted shipping containers. It was a brutal scene but better than sleeping under the viaducts. There was no room for weakness here; violence was second nature to any of the tranqs who needed a fix.

The city called it a housing project. The citizens called it the Grey Zone. Every lobo, zip head, punker, and non-conformist dropout was poured into this place and forced to survive. Society's waifs and strays had one thing in common: no parents. No one could remember where their parents disappeared to. It was as if someone had erased that part of their memory like an old optical disc drive. That was the thing about the Grey Zone. No one had a future or a past; there was only now.

In the distance: a metallic percussion desperate to breathe life into the Grey Zone. Axel slapped the ground harder and rolled towards it. One thing about survival was that you need friends to do it. Axel was

4

fortunate to have some that were still able-bodied and helpful.

Axel ground around a corner, where a skate-punk with a girl's soft features and a man's hardened expression pounded a beat on some rusted oil drums with two pieces of cut-off pipe. This was Scratch, an androgyne percussion expert and one of the toughest health food freaks Axel ever knew. Scratch had fright-wig spiked hair, dirty black clothes, and a cigarette hanging from their lips.

"Scratch! Scratch!" Axel yelled as he skidded to a stop next to the makeshift drum kit. "Stop that, Scratch! If you're not part of the problem, you're the solution!"

Scratch didn't stop. They kept smashing out the beat that reverberated in their brain, made it a reality.

"You jackoff!" Axel cried.

Scratch tried to ignore Axel, but he wouldn't let up: "Cut that shit out! Cut it out!

Cut that shit out, Scratch!"

Scratch stopped, and the dead silence of the Grey Zone seeped back into the soundtrack.

"Uh oh, you've been rolling around downtown again, Axel," Scratch said in a raspy voice that lived up to their name. "Sucking up nitrites and twitching."

Axel screwed his face up at this.

"Here," Scratch added. "This will make you feel better." Scratch handed Axel a corroded section of old pipe. Axel inspected it with disdain. Scratch returned to work, banging out a new metallic rhythm to rattle the containers of the Grey Zone.

Axel gripped the pipe hard. At least this had some life to it; this was a way to fight back against the banal broadcasting rays of EBN. *Fuck it. If you can't join 'em, beat 'em.*

"Goddamn Microwave hell!" Axel bellowed,

beating the nearest oil drum with the pipe, adding to Scratch's sounds. As the urban music bounced around the Grey Zone, it acted like a signal to the third member of Axel and Scratch's group.

Young Razoreus, slinked from his shipping container. An edgy kid, full of deviant hormones who, like Scratch, was an expert shoplifter and all-purpose vandal, Razoreus was around twelve-years-old. Maybe. Nobody knew how old he was exactly. Not even Razoreus. Not that age was something to bother remembering.

Razoreus wore a ripped sleeveless denim jacket over psychedelic shirt and pants, and had red spiked hair. He was street-smart, knew his way around the Grey Zone, and could handle himself. Like everyone else, he had no parents; he had grown up fast. He heard Scratch's music and tore past burning barrels and the lingering down-and-outs to find them.

Razoreus joined his friends, kicking his deck to one side and grabbing another section of snapped-off metal pipe to add to the music. They all pounded defiantly together. It was an anthem for the Zoners in the Grey.

Their music grew, smashed, and crashed, until Scratch rebelled against their own music and kicked over the oil drum. Razoreus toppled the drum he was playing, and finally Axel overturned his barrel. It was time they all left; they had an important date to keep.

All three grabbed their decks and skated deeper into the Zone.

* * *

Axel, Razoreus, and Scratch took their music on the road, thrashing through the Grey Zone on their decks, running their metal pipes along containers, creating their own soundtrack. They dodged punkers, losers, and degenerates. They flew down to the graffitied mini half-pipe set up by the trading bays. Some other sketchy, goofy-foot skaters were using it. Razoreus and Scratch pushed past them and lifted off over the half-pipe. Axel laughed and slapped his gloved hands on the asphalt, picking up speed.

The sun was beginning to set as the trio bullied their boards out of the housing slums of the Grey Zone towards the Thrash Bin Club. The three were going to watch the one guy none of them would forget, the one guy that would change everything: Orpheus.

INCOMING OVIDEO IN THREE...
TWO...

While with his songs, Orpheus,
the bard of the Grey Zone,
allured the trees, the savage animals,
and even the insensate rocks,
to follow him.

3

Everyone in the Zone liked Orpheus. He was the lead singer in a band called The Shredders. Axel, Razoreus, and Scratch would go see them every chance they could.

The Thrash Bin Club consisted of eighteen shipping containers welded together, painted black inside, and sprayed neon outside. Real music – thrashing, rocking and punking – wasn't underground anymore, it was subterranean.

The Thrash Bin Club was one of the last beacons to subvert the banality. There was a burly Zoner at the door, a hard-ass that gave any non-paying customers a hard time. Axel, Razoreus, and Scratch knew this, but not having money didn't stop them. They could always find a way to rock like rabid dogs. The big Zoner left the door open so they could watch from outside. Razoreus gave him a nod of appreciation; Axel wanted to tell the Zoner to blow it out his ass, but he kept his thoughts to himself.

The place was packed with every type of Zoner imaginable, all hollering for Orpheus. When Orpheus stepped on stage into a red spotlight, there was a sudden silence. Orpheus was tall, good-looking, a striking presence on stage, decked out in a psychedelic shirt, carrying a battered red guitar covered in duct tape. Orpheus was The Real Deal, a genuine alternative to the EBN-sanctioned music in a wasteland of predictability. The kids could relate to Orpheus: he didn't know where his parents had gone either. He raged against the oppressive world outside with every fiber of his being.

"Okay," said Orpheus into the mic. "One more and we gotta go." The crowd cheered as his voice boomed through the PA system. "Can we have a projection, please?"

An old 16mm reel showing worms writhing on a white background bloomed on the wall behind The Shredders.

"There's an old saying: nobody loves me — everybody hates me," Orpheus announced with attitude. "Guess I'll go eat worms."

Orpheus's girl, Eurydice, smiled wryly from a small go-go stage to his left. She was a petite brunette with brown, passionate eyes that could burn a hole in your soul. She dressed up every night to watch Orpheus play. Tonight, she wore a tight black dress adorned with all her best silver trinkets and chains.

Eurydice was a shining beacon of beauty in a wash of repressive RF rays. Orpheus was as sharp as a closed-circuit transmission in the gloom of the Grey Zone. The pair complemented each other, and their love was an example of perfect port-to-port connection in a sea of static. Everyone knew they had met years ago and supported each other through the bad and the worst. Together, they could wipe away all the Grey Zone's negative vibes for everyone: their love was the key.

"Go eat worms!" Orpheus shouted into the mic,

smiling at his love. "Don't do it! That's just the saying!"

Eurydice beamed at Orpheus.

Orpheus began to rock his guitar, and The Shredders fell into tune, cranking out their own brand of new-wave psychedelia. The crowd ate it up and went wild. Eurydice gyrated a seductive dance.

Linus, manager of Orpheus and The Shredders, gave a big thumbs-up from his side of the stage, almost dislodging his red-rimmed glasses from his face in excitement.

Orpheus began to sing in his signature deep, dreamy tone.

> *"A walking corpse,*
> *a life made cold,*
> *it cuts me,*
> *it cuts me to the bone.*
> *I want to touch you,*
> *but your skin is growing hard,*
> *I know you can't feel a thing*
> *There's fire in the ice!"*

Outside, Axel, Razoreus, and Scratch moshed against the club's cold metal walls. Axel rocked his deck back and forth, then lifted the front end and smashed it down over and over — *bang bang bang* — as Orpheus drank in the crowd's zeal and belted out his lyrics.

> *"Oh, you never lose control;*
> *you never let go.*
> *And if you squirm,*
> *you've got to be a worm!"*

The Shredders' longhaired drummer, Ronald,

pounded with ferocity as Amy, the bass player, aggressively pumped her strings. The band sounded razor sharp.

Like an invisible specter, a cold chill wisped past Axel and the others. Razoreus shivered like something had walked over his grave. They all saw it then; something with the complexion of a corpse slithered from one of the club's darkened corners. It was EBN's vampire video scout, camera pressed to its eye, roaming the Grey Zone to capture some poor, unsuspecting soul and trap them in a 4:3 frame. It was whispered that EBN occasionally sent their ghouls into the Grey Zone. When they did, people disappeared.

The Video Vampire was among the higher-ups, a talent scout, and an EBN producer. There were rumors there was something special in the Thrash Bin Club and the Video Vampire wanted to capture it on tape. He drifted through the crowd as if his feet didn't touch the floor. The heat-seeker on the lens of his camera captured a hot body in its viewfinder: Eurydice go-go dancing by the side of the stage.

Orpheus's expression dropped. Watching the ashen faced EBN ghoul focus Eurydice into his depth-of-field sent rage through his body.

The Video Vampire made it to the go-go podium, dropped to his knees, and filmed up at Eurydice, her image filled his viewfinder. He clearly liked that. EBN would like it, too.

Orpheus continued his song, desperate to ignore the attention the Video Vampire paid Eurydice.

> *"You're made of lava;*
> *you're made of ice.*
> *But I can't help you;*
> *there's a hunger in your eyes."*

13

Eurydice stared into the Video Vampire's camera fixed on her. Behind the lens, the pale ghoul grinned, and a chill carved its way through her body. Other revelers in the club begged the camera's attention. They crowded around her legs as she danced on her little podium. None of them cared if the Video Vampire stole their image, but Eurydice did.

Sweat formed on Orpheus's brow. He tried to compose himself and continued to sing.

> *"You never lose control;*
> *you never let go.*
> *And if you gonna squirm,*
> *you gotta be a worm!"*

Hands from the crowd grabbed for Eurydice, turning her expression to anguish. She tried to ignore the attention, but everything was getting worse: the groping crowd, the leering lens of the camera, and the dead face behind it. Her panic grew. She turned to Orpheus, but a rough hand from the crowd shot up and yanked her back to face the camera. Orpheus watched her mouth his name, her voice lost to The Shredders' music.

The Video Vampire wore a blank expression as he slithered closer to Eurydice, zooming and focusing and framing her fearful face.

That was enough.

Orpheus leaped from the stage and swung the un-dead-looking son-of-a-bitch away from Eurydice, and became the star of the Video Vampire's frame. The white-faced fucker didn't even flinch when Orpheus curled his right fist and drew back, ready to smash its face to flinders.

Axel watched all this from outside the club doors and cried, *"Yeahhhh!"* wanting the EBN asshole's shattering teeth to be the next instrument Orpheus played.

Another hand shot through the club's crowd and gripped tightly onto Orpheus's drawn fist. Manager Linus tried to speak sanity. "Orpheus, don't break the guy's face; it's not worth it!" he cried, his glasses almost steaming up with worry. He'd heard the stories and knew not to fuck with these EBN deadheads.

Orpheus listened, backed off, and then plucked Eurydice from her podium. "You don't have to do this," he said softly, taking her in his arms. Their eyes met, and that glow they generated in each other's presence returned. Orpheus grabbed his guitar, linked hands with Eurydice, and ran through the crowd to the club's front door.

The Video Vampire just watched as they went; he had Eurydice captured on his tape. That was enough for now. Until a decision had been made...

Orpheus burst through the club's front door, pushing Razoreus and Scratch to one side and almost spilling over Axel.

"Hey, Orpheus, nice work!" Scratch praised in their scratchy voice.

"Yeah, right — see you later," Orpheus replied as he rushed Eurydice away from the club, without sparing a moment for the trio.

"Yeah, right — see *you* later," Scratch rasped back, unimpressed. "Why is he so bent out of shape?"

"Ah, he's got a bug up his ass," Axel moaned, sad the night was over, sad Orpheus didn't blast the Video Vampire to the next plane of existence.

To the cheering crowd inside the Thrash Bin Club, it seemed like Orpheus had it made, a hot band and a hot dancer chick. But on this night, things were starting to get weird.

They were about to get weirder.

4

Later, the trio wanted some laughs to blow away the cobwebs of the heavy scene at the Thrash Bin Club. It was time for a little search-and-destroy mission. They crept to the border of the Grey Zone, to Rice's Auto Salvage, acres of spare parts, Heaven for all the junkers that rusted in peace.

At this time of night, owner Old Man Rice was always holed up in his little shack at the heart of the yard. He had security that patrolled the place, but they were as useless as a snooze button on a smoke alarm.

A TV glow came from the dirty window of Old Man Rice's shack. Axel, Razoreus, and Scratch moved closer. The able-bodied pair lifted Axel and propped him on a pile of tires to spy inside. It was then they stumbled on this weird new TV show, and their world changed forever.

Inside was Old Man Rice, slumped into a worn-out chair, wearing his dirty denim cap and work shirt, looking tired from a hard day of stripping shit-box cars to do anything but stare at the screen. The TV day was over, and the tube had Old Glory blowing as the National Anthem played. Old Man Rice gulped down a beer. Then, an odd interference aggressively strangled the TV's image, stabbing at the flying flag until wavering grain, like a sea of analog maggots, filled the screen.

A new image with dreary droning soundtrack now dominated TV A digital image: a satellite with a hooked antenna beamed devil-red rays into the black void background.

The trio of Zoners pressed in closer to watch.

A whispering voice slinked through the set's tiny speaker.

"Don't touch that dial. Welcome, late-night viewers. It's time for your favorite video narcotic. From the underworld entertainment capital, the Euthanasia Broadcast Network Presents: Praise The Ray. *And now here are your hosts, Hades and Persephone Hecata."*

A purple video eye projected onto the tube. Old Man Rice's eyes reflected the

screen, like he had tiny twin TVs embedded in his sockets.

Axel twitched as he stared at the video eye; he had an odd feeling that it was looking out of the screen as they were looking in.

The purple eye's digital retina dissolved to a crystal-clear image of a slick, pale-faced EBN ghoul wearing a flashy green and purple cloak. The EBN ghoul at the Thrash Bin Club was a Video Vampire. The face on screen belonged to the Hi-Def Dracula of the EBN pack: Hades Hecata.

Axel, Razoreus, and Scratch wanted to rip away as fear coursed through their bodies. But they couldn't fight the video's effects pulling them closer with invisible transmitted teleplasms.

"Good evening, ladies and gentlemen," Hades said with all the charm of a serpent. *"And welcome to the world of sedate, where the subliminal meets the sublime. Sit*

back, relax, and let the cathode rays fill your soul, as we share the ministry of somnolence."

The image cut to a girl wearing sparkling jewelry and too much makeup: Persephone Hecata. Her eyes bulged, blood-red lips parted, exposing teeth like a row of China tombstones. *"Praise the ray!"* she hissed in ecstasy.

Old Man Rice was transfixed to the tube, his mouth gaping.

"Let yourself be comfortable," Hades said silkily. *"Give yourself to the ray. The ray is so comforting, so soothing. Let yourself absorb the ray into every pore of your body."*

Scratch had enough of this shit. They broke away and wandered into the junkyard.

Persephone Hecata cut back on the screen, and Axel and Razoreus watched Old Man Rice watch her on his TV.

"The light from the ray is the beautiful mystery of waves and particles and particles and waves, becoming waves of parts and parts of waves," Persephone said in a dreamy, lulling voice. *"Blending into little wave-icles of lightning bugs washing over you and cleansing and healing you."* The camera slowly zoomed into her face. Persephone, who looked attractive mid-shot, had a morbid corpse-like sheen in a close-up. *"As you breathe in, observe the teeny, weeny bits of microwave radiation manifest in your being."*

Razoreus slumped into the window, pressing his face against the pane. He felt mesmerized by Persephone's words, too. Axel, hardened to media manipulation, fought the feeling of the screen taking possession of his consciousness, but he had to admit, this shit was good.

"As you breathe out," Persephone went on, seduc-

tively exhaling, *"feel the warm glow. So soothing. So relaxing. So... give yourself to the ray..."*

Scratch found an old metal rod and began playing percussive passages on racks of spare parts. Hitting hubcaps and mashing mufflers, the underground rhythm started again — the soundtrack of the Grey Zone.

Axel and Razoreus snapped their heads in the makeshift music's direction, torn away from the hypnotic tube.

Little did they know the distraction came just in time.

As Axel and Razoreus watched Scratch smash out a metallic beat behind them, *Praise The Ray*'s electromagnetic signal went into overdrive. Persephone's eyes rolled back in her skull as the EBN satellites went into complete power overload. Old Man Rice's screen had become a video vortex pulling at his essence. The rays projected from the screen, patched into his soul, and yanked it free from his flesh. EBN had become the network of the OBE — out of body experience — and if Axel and Razoreus had turned back and looked through Old Man Rice's window, they would not be able to describe what they saw.

Old Man Rice seemed to split. A translucent version of him, emerged from his body, like a cheap special effect, a video ghost, drawn towards the TV, enticed by Persephone's siren call. It looked for all the world as if his spirit simply left, abandoning its meat housing, to be sucked into the screen and eaten by the scan lines, forever falling through a video dream of sizzling static.

Razoreus ran to Scratch and thrashed out metallic music with a snapped-off brake line. Axel laughed and slapped his thigh with a gloved hand. Their music gave him hope that one day everyone would give up the boob tube and get back to basics.

Razoreus had to get the hypnotized feeling from his head. He fought against it, rebelled against it in his mind, and then stomped off to an old jalopy to his left. He yanked the driver's side door off its hinges, climbed up, jumped up and down on the roof, caving it in. He threw his deck at the hood, laughing as it bounced off. Then, he jumped on the hood, put a massive dent into its center. He let his anger flow through him, picking up his deck and smashing out the jalopy's fogged-up headlights. Scratch followed suit, climbed on the beat-up car's roof, and thrashed it with their deck.

"Break that sucker down!" Axel bellowed, dropping from his propped-up position to his board.

Scratch stood on the roof and announced in their raspy voice: "Today's used cars are better than ever before. We offer five hundred years — fifty-million-mile protection. The rust never sleeps; today, the pride is back. If you can find a better deal, thrash it!"

Scratch raised their deck high and brought it down fast, obliterating the jalopy's windscreen to splintered shards.

"Boot it!" Axel yelled ecstatically. "Jesus, Buddha, bust it!"

A voice bellowed from the junkyard's darkness; a flashlight beam burst across the crumpled car.

"Hey! What are you doing?"

Fuck. A security guard.

"Hey! Let's get out of here!" Axel hollered, spinning himself around on his board. Razoreus and Scratch fled from the destroyed car, skating away at full speed, towing Axel along to help him escape.

The guard couldn't catch them. He didn't even get a look at them in the junkyard's gloom. Giving up, he returned to the main office and found Old Man Rice's limp body in front of a snowy screen.

They used to say watching too much TV gave you square eyes. With the EBN network, watching too much *Praise The Ray* left you with a cold corpse.

RF didn't stand for "radio frequency" anymore.

Not that they realized it, but for Orpheus, Axel, Razoreus, and Scratch, RF stood for "Really Fucked."

Soon, they would find out why.

An EBN Ovideo scroll, a message for all,
seeking prey:

> *Veiled in a saffron mantle, through the air*
> *unmeasured, after the strange wedding,*
> *Hymenaeus departed swiftly for Ciconian*
> *   land;*
> *regardless and not listening*
> *to the voice of tuneful Orpheus.*

5

The Grey Zone: at the Marginal Way Village Housing Project, Orpheus sat on his bed and strummed his beaten-up guitar. The sound reverberated around the shipping container he called home; a carousel lamp slowly spun beside the bed, projecting calming pastels, softening the cold metal walls.

Orpheus didn't have much in the way of worldly possessions, but what he kept meant something. On a cabinet was a pile of cassettes, and above them hung a poster of the man who changed Orpheus's life.

When he was thirteen, Orpheus had been boarding around an old vacant housing project — a place that promised the future of affordable housing that no one could afford — when he came across the derelict pad of a long-dead sixties throwback. The trashed junk inside held little interest to the other Zoners with him, but there was something about the poster in the bedroom, of the black man with a headband, that called to him. There was a life to his eyes that was a rare trait in Orpheus's worn-out world. Moving closer, inspecting the poster, Orpheus found the collection of cassettes, each one's case bearing the visage of the man from the poster: Jimi Hendrix.

Orpheus instinctively understood he was supposed to have the tapes. Everything became apparent when he took them back to his container and played them. Jimi's psychedelic mix of rock and rhythm and blues painted the Grey Zone in a rainbow of bright oily colors. Orpheus never had parents, never had a chance, never had hope, but he would always have Hendrix, and a little piece of Jimi played in his soul.

Only one other person touched Orpheus this way. In front of him, Eurydice in a kimono seductively stepped out from behind an old dressing screen. She swayed in front of Orpheus, hoping he would make a move, but he only smiled slightly and continued to play.

Eurydice reached out, grabbed the guitar from Orpheus, and leaned it against the bedside cabinet. Orpheus gazed at Eurydice as she passed him the silky belt of her kimono. He slowly pulled the kimono open, to see the familiar soft body inside, when Eurydice yanked the belt back, pulling Orpheus to his feet. They held each other tight. Slowly spinning in each other's arms. Her love was the only other thing that gave Orpheus's existence a splash of color.

They both sighed and fell back on the bed, Eurydice on top of Orpheus, teasing him with her kiss.

"You love to torture me," Orpheus said softly.

"Because you deserve it," Eurydice replied, looking deep into his eyes. "You need to be punished."

Orpheus grabbed Eurydice and quickly spun her to the bed, so he was on top of her. "What did I do?" he asked.

Eurydice continued the game. She grabbed Orpheus and spun him, pinning him back to the bed, and straddled him again. "Oh, that thrashing around making all that nasty racket."

She teased him again, moving in for a kiss and then dodging away. "Did you do that when you were growing up?"

"Ma'am, I've dedicated my life to the sound of metal insects screaming in a wall of oatmeal."

Eurydice laughed. Orpheus really did say the wildest things. "Since when?" she asked, playing with his guitar calloused hand.

"Oh, back in '86. The first band I ever played in was a speed metal Neo Detroit outfit with Direct Eye Marshall Stacks. They were called Latent Death Wish," Orpheus replied.

"Latent Death Wish?" Eurydice said. "Don't you think that name's cutting it too close?"

Orpheus laughed. "Oh, don't get serious on me. That was just a stupid marketing strategy for the corpse look-a-like crowd."

"The strategy didn't work, huh?" Eurydice said cockily, pinning Orpheus to the bed. "You're still alive, aren't you?"

Orpheus looked deeply into her eyes. "Try me."

Eurydice looked back; a connection made. "Do I have to?" she purred.

There was a tense pause, Eurydice edging her lips closer to Orpheus's.

"Do you want to?" Orpheus answered.

Eurydice felt a pulse of heat pass through her body.

Then they kissed.

The pair made love for over an hour. It was the perfect coupling. Their touch ignited the electricity that crackled for one another. When they were together like this, the whole wrecked world outside ceased to exist. There was only each other.

But, outside the Grey Zone, lurid eyes watched Eurydice.

6

Inside the cold, dead EBN tower, three foul faces leered at a glowing monitor in a darkened room. A haze of cigarette smoke lingered around them like the mist from a late-night graveyard. The Video Vampire's footage of Eurydice seductively dancing on her podium played on the screen. As she gyrated to Orpheus's music, Hades and Persephone Hecata watched with the pale-faced ghoul who filmed it, now wearing his producer's cap as he tried to convince them he'd found their new star.

"I hope you like this one," the Video Vampire muttered, eyes fixed on Eurydice's curves. "I think she would be great on the show."

Hades took a drag from his cigarette, his purple lips slowly sucking the butt.

They all paused to take in Eurydice. The Video Vampire showing the only emotion he knew: a perverted lust.

"She's got *greaattttt* moves," he hissed.

On-screen, the video reached the point where Orpheus jumped from the stage and manhandled the Video Vampire, rolling back his fist, ready to plant one on him.

Persephone's dull eyes lit up with desire. "He's not bad either." The words slithered from her blood-red lips.

"Yes, perhaps," said Hades. He stubbed out his cigarette and instantly lit another. "But you can never really tell on tape."

Hades admired Eurydice dancing as the Video Vampire backed out of the club. Then an idea caught in his mind and ran through his grey matter. "See, the proof is to see her dead… in person."

A morbid silence filled the small viewing room.

"We've got plenty of storage," the Video Vampire said, "and we need some fresh talent."

Hades took another drag from his cigarette.

The Video Vampire wanted her, needed her for the show, and for that, he had to convince Hades.

"It's absolutely critical to our growth," he said, trying to persuade the pair. "The Euthanasia Network has captured 85% of the population over seventy. Our programming is hardwired into every retirement and convalescent home in the country twenty-four hours a day. We've also got the trilateral corporate structure. But if we are going to expand our viewing addicts beyond the corporate crust, we need to reach out and put our finger on the main vein of the youth market. We need the heartbeat of America."

A hardened sneer grew on Hades' face.

Almost orgasmic, Persephone exclaimed, "That is it!"

"Do you think you can start with her?" Hades asked.

The Video Vampire pulled a rare smile. "I think we can build a program around her. With her, we can play *Peoria*."

Hades blew a long stream of smoke. "Get her," were the words that crept past Hades' lips.

Smug satisfaction crawled over the Video Vampire's face.

Hades reached for the remote, pointed it at the image of Eurydice on the screen, and reduced it to a pinpoint of light.

The screen faded to black.

7

In Orpheus's shipping container, soft electronic music played from a shoebox cassette deck Eurydice held in her hand. It was her turn to pick the music now. Orpheus always wanted rock; she wanted something with soul even if it was synthesized. Orpheus had filled an old metal tub with warm water and washed Eurydice's feet, softly soaping her toes and soles. He appreciated the hours she put in grooving to his music, and he would always show it by performing this ritual after his shows.

"Looks like you might have overdone it," Orpheus said softly, rubbing the torn flesh of a popped blister.

"Do I have any choice when the music is The Shredders?" Eurydice answered, giving him a slow wink.

Orpheus laughed, went back to washing her feet, and playfully bit her right foot.

Eurydice gasped and dropped the cassette deck. It rolled in the air, hitting the side of Orpheus's bed, before tumbling into the tin tub. A bright explosion erupted as the deck's electric innards were washed with water. A slight shock sparked through Eurydice's body, knocking her back on the bed.

Orpheus reached into the tub, grabbed the deck, and tossed it to one side.

Orpheus dove on top of Eurydice, staring into her frightened eyes. A foul thought traveled through Orpheus's mind: if the damn thing was plugged into the mains, he might have lost her.

Gone.

Dead.

Fried because of a pointless accident.

A new fear settled in Orpheus. He'd never considered life without Eurydice, and a cold dread clawed down his spine.

* * *

Later, outside the container, Orpheus warmed his hands over a fire he'd started in an old oil drum. He watched the reaching flames eat through the dried wood of an old pallet; tiny sparks travelled up into the night, spiriting around the darkness of the Grey Zone.

He hated the idea of life without Eurydice. It haunted his head like a ghost since the tape deck accident.

Suddenly, the sound of movement came from the shadows. Someone was watching him.

Scratch lunged from the gloom towards him.

"Hey, Orpheus," Scratch rasped. "Let's go hit the Safeway."

Orpheus had to give it to Scratch, they were one of the most consistent health food junkies he'd met.

"Sorry, I've got other plans," Orpheus replied.

Scratch's lips curled back, showing their clenched teeth in the red glow of the fire. What was with Orpheus these days? In the good old days, they would be out all-night breaking and entering every supermarket's back door for all the food they could find.

"Hey, we've got to stock up for the month," Scratch pleaded.

Orpheus turned back to the fire and stared into the flames. An existential understanding ate at him: there had to be a better life than this. Late-night burglarizing to snag healthy food snacks wouldn't cut it forever.

Scratch's anger turned to annoyance. "Come on, man. Don't go soft on me."

"Orpheus?" a soft voice called behind them. Eurydice stepped into the cold night air, wrapped in one of his oversized leather jackets. She curled into him, holding him tight, and Orpheus pulled her closer.

Scratch looked at them both with deep disappointment. Orpheus had become increasingly distant since he invited Eurydice into his life. The pair were inseparable, and because of their unity, Orpheus's friendship with Scratch, Axel, and Razoreus had drifted.

"You are going soft," Scratch hissed and disappeared into the darkness of the Grey Zone. Only the crackling sound of the dried-out timber burning in the old oil drum.

Orpheus didn't want to abandon his friends like this, but he wanted more than his past of boarding and breaking and entering with his old buds. It hurt jilting them this way, but things had to change. He stared at the flames, the dichotomy of his old life and his new life drilling into his mind.

"What do you think?" Eurydice said, looking deeply into Orpheus's eyes.

Orpheus stared back at the flames, contemplating his past, his future, and his present. Eurydice sensually squeezed his side and nuzzled against him.

He wanted this to be his future.

He wanted Eurydice forever.

"I'm ready for a change," he answered.

They had spoken about the future before, about forever, planning a life in late-night whispers that could only be dreams.

Or could they?

Sometimes, when you want dreams to become reality, you just have to do it. Go against the flow. Take the jump. Throw caution to the wind and say fuck it. Some things were worth taking a chance for.

Eurydice was worth everything and more.

She felt the same about Orpheus.

Eurydice smiled. "You ready?" she asked.

She was his love.

She was his forever.

"Let's do it," she whispered.

Eurydice moved into Orpheus and kissed him passionately.

Without saying a word, as the fire smoldered and crackled, giving light to the gloom of the Grey Zone, their bond twined tighter, and a decision was made without words.

It was time for a change.

Forever.

> Truly Hymeneus there
> was present during the festivities
> of Orpheus and Eurydice, but gave
> no happy omen, neither hallowed words
> nor joyful glances;
> and the torch he held would only sputter,
> fill the eyes with smoke,
> and cause no blaze while waving.
> The result of that sad wedding,
> proved more terrible
> than such foreboding fates.

END TRANSMISSION…

35

8

The sea of twinkling, colored lights from the upper residential districts mixed with the pollution from the industrial quarters of the Grey Zone, creating a blanket of neon in the night sky. It was the perfect backdrop — as perfect as perfect could be living in such bleak times — for the ceremony on top of the old disused parking lot.

A makeshift aisle had been constructed with hard-wired overhead bulbs. At the end of the aisle, a punk-rock priest with a crucifix earring and crucifix pins on his jacket, grinned at the couple in front of him. It was rare for a spark of happiness in the Grey Zone. It gave the padre a little hope inside his soul.

There was excitement among the small crowd that had attended: smiles on faces, electricity in the air. *This is what it's all about*, thought the priest as he spoke, looking at the couple before him. *Love — real love.* Looking at the pair, he could tell this was no half-baked impulse marriage.

Orpheus loved Eurydice.

Eurydice loved Orpheus.

And now, they would be together forever.

Orpheus was dressed in his best pink leopard-print jacket, and Eurydice in her best floral dress. They looked perfect. The couple's joy spread to Eurydice's best friend and bridesmaid, Aphaea, another go-go dancer from the club. Manager Linus was his best man.

A train blared off in the distance as the punk-rock priest caught a breath and continued his sermon. "And now, by the power vested in me by the state of mind, incorporated within ephemeral boundaries known as the Grey Zone, I hereby pronounce you husband and wife."

Orpheus and Eurydice's soulful stare into each other's eyes broke momentarily as they smiled.

This was it.

Together forever.

The small crowd attending all hollered and cheered. The Shredders were there, as were a handful of friends from the Grey Zone. Axel, Scratch, and Razoreus all watched on.

In all his however many years on the planet, Razoreus had never considered the kind of happiness Orpheus had found. It was an alien feeling in his mind, but seeing the pair together unlocked something within him. He'd miss Orpheus being a part of their crew but understood what he'd found with Eurydice. Maybe one day he'd find love.

Yeah, right. Get a grip.

Orpheus and Eurydice were still looking at one another, caught up in the moment. A wry smile broke over the punk-rock priest's face. "You can go ahead and kiss each other," he said, amused.

Slowly, they did, and another cheer broke out. Razoreus's cynical outlook shattered as their lips met. "Yeahhhhhh!" he cheered as they kissed, clapping as hard as he could.

Orpheus and Eurydice pulled away from the

punk-rock priest, and Orpheus held his hand to him. "Thanks a lot."

"It's my pleasure," said the punk-rock priest, shaking Orpheus's hand tightly. "Congratulations. I'm sorry your folks can't be around to see this. They'd be very happy for you."

"Thank you," Orpheus said, slightly sad they couldn't attend. Not that he'd be alone in this feeling; two-thirds of the attendees had no idea where their parents were.

"*Muchas gracias!*" Linus moved towards Eurydice in his usual dorky way. "Let me be the first," he joked, planting his puckered lips on Eurydice's cheek. He let out a geeky laugh that made everyone crack up. Even Axel and Scratch chuckled, and that was rare.

"All right!" Linus announced, "Now I have procured some of that incredible punch for the occasion, so shall we let the fun begin?"

Loud electronic music blared through speakers set up around the parking lot roof. Linus had put on quite a spread: real wood tables and chairs, unstained tablecloths, glasses that weren't splintered with cracks — tonight felt like the real deal.

Orpheus and Eurydice made their way to the main table. A waiter in a tacky blue suit pulled a chair out for Eurydice. That's when she noticed his skin's putrid blue pigmentation. A shiver ran down her spine.

No. It must just be a blue hue from the polluted sky, right?

Or the cheap suit tinting his face in the limited light, right?

You're being paranoid, she told herself.

Ignore it — Ignore it — Ignore it.

Eurydice looked up at the waiter's face. He had the same grey, undead face and blank, drawn-on eyes as the Video Vampire that stalked her in the club. Eurydice quickly looked away and whispered to Orpheus. "Where did we get these caterers?"

Orpheus stared up at the waiter standing behind them. The guy looked practically propped up, stiff and with the emotion of a fence post. Orpheus laughed. "You know Linus and his weird deals; they probably came with the place."

Eurydice smiled slightly and nodded. Orpheus leaned in and kissed her. Eurydice's bridesmaid, Aphaea, appeared behind them and leaned down, her smile as wide as the horizon. "Congratulations!"

Eurydice hugged her friend tightly. "Thank you!"

Orpheus could see the happiness on Eurydice's face and thanked her friend, too.

Linus bopped his head to the music and loomed over the catering table, grabbing the ladle from the punch bowl, concerned but determined to hide it. If only the other caterer hadn't pulled out at the last minute. Why had they sounded so panicked when they'd called to say they couldn't make it? Well, at least these guys were fifty credits cheaper, even if they had all the charisma of a satisfied undertaker.

Before he could pour a glass of the bright green liquid, he looked at the block of ice in the center of the bowl: it had been carved to the perfect shape of a skull. Linus looked up at the waitress behind the table ready to give her one of his so-bad-it's-terrible lines ("A skull at a wedding! That's about as appropriate as an accordion player at a deer hunt!")

The grey-faced waitress stared at him with doll-like eyes, like an escapee from the morgue. There was no emotion, no expression, nothing. So he said nothing.

Picking up a knife, Linus tapped the glass of toxic-looking punch, sending out an irritating appeal.

"Revelers! Revelers! May I have your attention, please? I would like to propose a toast to the bride and groom."

A small round of applause came from the crowd. Linus raised his glass to them.

"To the bride and groom! May their love be invincible, inexhaustible, *relentlessssss*," Linus laughed like a goof, "totally consuming, and, of course, eternal." He raised his glass higher. *"Prost! Prost!"* The gathering of friends cheered and raised their glasses. "Now!" Linus announced. "Come here, you two! I want to give you a wedding present!" He picked a gift wrapped in black paper tied with a pink bow and approached Orpheus and Eurydice. "Come on, come on!"

Orpheus and Eurydice laughed and got up from their table as Linus lured them over with the gift.

"That's it, come on! Come on!"

Linus offered the box to them both. "The perfect gift for the musician and the dancer."

The pair took the gift and examined the odd, almost V-shaped box. Eurydice lifted the lid, revealing a compact six-stringed instrument with a white faceplate and polished copper trim. It looked like a guitar with no neck and all body.

Razoreus ran over and blurted, "Whoa! What is it?"

Linus straightened up and proudly said, "The Gibsonian Lyre-Axe guitar, designed by Mr. Jimi Hendrix."

Orpheus's jaw dropped. No way. It was myth that this thing existed. Not in a million years could he have imagined it being true or being given one, especially by Linus.

Orpheus took the instrument from the box like he was handing a diamond. Linus had as much edge as a circle and the personality of a game show host cross-bred with a used car salesman. Still, this... He'd really gone above and beyond.

"Only three prototypes were ever built," Linus said, "And it comes complete with this mini electronic interface system." He took a small black device from the gift's packaging and passed it to Orpheus.

It hit Orpheus as he held the instrument: the technology he was holding was way beyond what was available when Jimi died. "When did Hendrix do this?" Orpheus asked.

"Ah, well," Linus awkwardly responded, clearing his throat to sound more confident, "So the story goes: He got together with this guy, Mr. Paisley Pattern. Their objective was to create the ultimate power chord machine to alter and elevate human consciousness."

Orpheus gave Eurydice a look. Was he being serious?

"But, but, but," Linus went on, "Jimi died before they could work out all the bugs. Gibson never got it past the prototype phase, and then Mr. Pattern disappeared with the design plans. Poof! Spooky, huh? So, who knows what this will do in the hands of the right musician? In any case, it remains a collector's item and should make a valuable addition to your family home entertainment center. So, fire it up, *bubbela*! Let's see what you can do!"

Orpheus took a black guitar strap from the gift box, attached it to the Lyre-Axe, and hung it around his neck. He inspected the instrument, working out the mini electronic interface system. Attached to his left wrist was a strap, and a tiny amp and synthesizer. A small copper tube unplugged from the rear of the triangular instrument, and he placed over his left index finger. Orpheus quickly figured out how the

Lyre-Axe worked. When you played its strings, the corresponding chords could be achieved based on the distance between the Lyre-Axe to the copper tube. It then transmitted to the mini electronic interface system and was amplified. It was an all-in-one compact portable guitar and amp.

This was wild. He couldn't believe he was holding it. Where the hell had Linus gotten this thing? Orpheus pushed a button, and the instrument's faceplate lit up with a white neon glow and a low droning hum. He pressed a button on the electronic interface system and an electronic drumbeat began to play.

This thing was *wild*.

He plucked at the Lyre-Axe's strings and, with an instinct he never knew he had, instantly mastered the obscure instrument. His fingers moved as if they weren't his own, understanding how to achieve each chord automatically, and he played along with the electronic beat. The music flowed as if Jimi himself possessed Orpheus. The Lyre-Axe's sound was a mix of surrealist psychedelia played with a Sitar at the world's edge. Back in the sixties, they would have said that this was Far Out. It was Far Out, all right, almost on another plane of existence.

As Orpheus played, feeling the music flow through him, the vibration of the strings amplified and seemed to blur the reality around it, churning the air into a vortex of glowing light. There was something special about the Lyre-Axe, and it flowed to Orpheus's fingers and reverberated through his body.

Razoreus looked on, hypnotized by the Lyre-Axe's kaleidoscopic light show. Linus was the same way.

Eurydice, too, was so taken by the music Orpheus created that she was moved to dance. Like she'd never danced before. She danced across the parking lot as if gliding on air, writhing and gyrating, moving to the concrete barrier at the roof's edge, climbing on a small platform. She started spinning and spinning as if she were back on her go-go podium.

As Eurydice danced and Orpheus grooved. Swaying to the intoxicating tunes, no one noticed another grey-faced waiter moving through the crowd with purpose. He held a tray with what looked like fortune cookies. There was nothing fortunate about them. Oozing inside each one was a live writhing worm.

Nobody gave a damn. All attention was on Orpheus as he played the Gibsonian.

The ghoulish waiter stepped up on the platform next to Eurydice as she spun closer and closer to the parking lot's edge. She stopped spinning — *do it!* — reached for a fortune cookie — *take it!* — grabbed it — *eat it!* — and took a bite.

Shock hit Eurydice's face as the cookie's squirming inside coiled around her tongue. She gagged and spat out the gross grub to the ground.

The grey-faced ghoul dropped the platter down and slid a cold hand down Eurydice's top, groping her breasts. Rage ran through Eurydice. She slapped the ghoul straight across the face with a satisfying snap. He didn't flinch; he just stared at her with pus-yellow eyes.

From behind him, the other grey-faced ghoul — the one who stood behind her and Orpheus at the table — crept up with a huge weapon in his hand. A gun with a barrel made from a TV tube, with an oversized eye at its end.

The ghoul pulled the trigger, and a high-powered blast of condensed cathode rays burst out, forming a three-dimensional graphic of the purple eye logo from EBN's *Praise The Ray* that hung in the air, hypnotizing Eurydice to the spot.

The tube gun crackled with power, the cathode rays intensified as a huge radioactive burst enveloped Eurydice and burned her flesh.

She screamed, stumbled, toppled backward over the parking lot's concrete barrier, twisting and turning in the air, three stories down, until...

The sickening crack of fragile bones on hardened concrete. The sound echoed.

Eurydice's screaming stopped.

So did the music. Orpheus ran in the direction of the sickening sound.

That's when the party ended.

That's when the nightmare began.

A cruel Ovideo played to anyone watching. The cruelest one yet. The side-scrolling blue letters without sympathy or judgment:

> *While through the grass delighted Naiads*
> > *wandered*
> *with the bride,*
> *a serpent struck its venomed tooth*
> *in her soft ankle*
> *— and she died.*

> *After, the bard of Rhodope had mourned,*
> *and filled the highs of heaven*
> *with the moans of his lament.*

45

9

Orpheus stared over the parking lot's barrier. Eurydice's broken doll's body lay on the cold concrete.

Orpheus shook his head.

No.

This can't be happening.

He wasn't aware that the grey, ghoul-faced waiters and the waitress had vanished from the party.

Linus ran to Orpheus, and he too looked over the edge. "Jesus... Oh, Jesus," were the only words he could croak.

Axel, Scratch, and Razoreus followed, as did the other wedding guests, their jaws hanging in shock at the sight of Eurydice's body below.

"Oh no!"

"Shit!"

"What happened!"

Then, from the shadows below, all three grey-faced waiters emerged and flocked around Eurydice like a pack of vultures in tacky blue suits. Without a glance at the crowd above, they plucked Eurydice's limp body from the ground and took off with her into the night.

Orpheus gritted his teeth. Anguish turned to anger. If only he'd listened to Eurydice – if only he wasn't caught up in their happy moment and listened when she tried to tell him the staff were bad news. No time for that now. Orpheus shoved through the crowd of attendees, almost tripping over Axel.

"Get those fucks!" Axel cried.

Orpheus fully intended to.

Orpheus bolted down the levels of the parking lot. If only he had his deck. He would be on them in no time if he had his deck! No time for wishful thinking now. Faster than he could think, Orpheus reached the spot where Eurydice had fallen.

One of her earrings shimmered in a silver beam of moonlight as Orpheus barreled after her abductors. His feet pounded the ground hard and fast, his fists tight, the veins in his arms cording around muscles.

He ran past old derelict warehouses, shifting in and out of shadows so fast it was as if sections of reality had been edited out, like frames of a film.

Ahead, he could see the three grey-faced ghouls carting Eurydice off. He had to get her, no matter what.

Sweating, muscles aching, Orpheus never lost speed, never slowed a beat. He was gaining on them; he could do this. Nothing was as important.

The girl ghoul ran to a grey-painted door of a warehouse, fumbled at the handle, and wrenched it wide open. The other two bearing Eurydice slid into the darkness beyond the frame, disappearing inside. The door slammed shut with a booming finality.

A sudden sickness ate inside Orpheus's stomach. He reached the door and yanked at the handle. Locked — as if it could never be opened. He fought against this reality, grunting and straining, begging and swearing. The damn door wouldn't budge.

Orpheus thumped the door with his fists. "Eurydice! Eurydice!"

Silence from the other side.

Orpheus stepped away from the door. The dull feeling of defeat knifed through his heart.

Eurydice… where are yo—

Any sign of sorrow vanished as he looked down at the Lyre-Axe. It was glowing, humming, warping the air around it, blurring reality with its shimmering light.

Inspiration hit Orpheus like an eighteen-wheeler.

He tilted the Lyre-Axe left and right, manipulating the generated glow into a beam. He moved the instrument some more, curving the tip of the luminosity into a pin-pointed pyramid of light. Instinct touched him again, telling him how to play the instrument. He understood this was the right thing to do; this would work. Orpheus thrust forward, directing the manipulated glow into the door's handle. A shower of sparks erupted around Orpheus. He looked away, closing his eyes tight from the explosion. An odd electronic whine screeched out into the air. Orpheus opened his eyes. The handle was mangled and bowed, and the once-solid door slowly crept open.

His new wife's name whispered through his lips.

"Eurydice."

Orpheus peered into the deep darkness beyond the jamb, swallowed hard, and dove inside.

10

The door snapped shut behind him, locking tight. Everything was pitch black, like stepping into an empty void. Orpheus looked left and right, heart thumping in his chest. He had to find her — *had to*. He walked forward, his footsteps echoing. There had to be a way out.

Ahead, a tiny pinprick of light appeared. Orpheus ran towards it, his breath ragged with fear. The pinprick morphed to an oblong of fluorescent light — a doorframe. As he drew nearer, he slowed, studied what was beyond the door, and gasped.

How could he have been so ignorant? Why hadn't he put two and two together? The video of the vampire at the Thrash Bin Club and the grey-faced ghouls at their wedding all added to one thing: EBN. He was walking into the dull grey reception area of EBN, where another of their pale-faced lackeys tapped away at a computer screen.

He stepped through the door onto a freshly laid carpet, turned to his right, and inspected the security camera mounted on the wall, aware that as he investigated the lens, somewhere, another ghoul looked back. Orpheus felt like a deer entering a lion's den.

He had to be cool to get Eurydice back. What the hell did these zombies want with her?

Play it cool.

Find out.

Orpheus stepped to the reception desk, swallowed, ready to ask questions when the pale receptionist barked at him with all the personality of an android: "Name?"

He didn't have time to think. Orpheus shrugged and told the truth.

"Orpheus."

The pale-faced receptionist punched his name into the computer and pressed enter. Then robotically asked, "Last?"

Orpheus shrugged again. "Hellenbach."

A dull female voice droned over the intercom as the pale-faced receptionist typed in Orpheus's last name.

"Jim Bakker, line three, please. Jim Bakker, line three."

The receptionist continued to type.

Orpheus looked around nervously. What the hell was he trying to do? Why did he give them his real name? He had to do something – anything to progress further into the building.

He jumped as the receptionist's dot matrix printer lurched to life, slowly printing a page of text. The pale-faced receptionist stared at Orpheus, eyeing him up and down. Orpheus held his gaze.

"A bit early, aren't you?" The pale-faced receptionist asked.

Orpheus shifted on the spot uncomfortably. All he could do was shrug.

The pale-faced receptionist tore off the printout, placed it in a manila folder of other papers, and passed it to Orpheus. "Please go down the hall to room 3A."

He went to say something to the pale-faced receptionist, but the phone rang, and she picked it up. "EBN. We bring good things to death."

She waved Orpheus on.

Had they mistaken him for someone else, or had they been waiting for his arrival? Orpheus didn't know. Right now, it didn't matter; all he had to do was go deeper into the building to find his love.

11

A dead-looking girl with blank, drawn-on eyes,
shuffled past Orpheus in a long grey hallway. *What
were they doing to people here?*

Another EBN security camera watched his every
move as he continued into the building.

A voice bellowed out: *"Please bring your files to debriefing. William Casey to debriefing."*

It was only the intercom.

Orpheus quickly flicked through the printed files
in his hand. Somehow, EBN had printed a journal of
every moment of his life until the moment he entered
the building. He turned back to the document's first
page; it was headed: **Memories.**

Memories?

The manila folder and memory files had signifi-
cance; he could feel they had some kind of power as
he held them in his hands. They weren't just paper, or
words on a page; they had a symbiotic association
with his soul, a tethered connection to his very being.
A sickening worry clenched his guts. What if all his
memories were to end the second he walked into the
building?

What the hell was EBN doing?

Orpheus walked until he reached the end of the hall; it split off to the left and right.

Where was he going? What was he going to do?

A loud mechanical chewing sound came from the right. Orpheus followed it.

* * *

In Styx Room 3A, an elderly, grey-faced ghoul in a white lab coat fed paperwork into an EBN-branded shredder. Thin strands of destroyed data curled on the floor as the machine did its work. The entire room was a spaghetti junction of files that had been fed through the machine. Bales of eaten paperwork propped up every wall in the place. The elderly ghoul reached beside the shredder, picked up an old, rusted putting iron and knocked a worn-out golf ball into an EBN regulation mug. If the higher-ups knew he was having fun outside the specified hours, it could mean big trouble. It was a good thing that anyone barely-

There was a knock at the counter door, and it opened.

Quickly, the elderly ghoul hid his putter by his side and turned back to the machine, pretending to concentrate on his work. "Just leave it on the counter, please."

"Okay, but first, I've got a question," Orpheus replied.

The elderly ghoul didn't recognize the voice; it sounded too full of life to be one of the usual EBN drones. But there was something very familiar about it...

"What's that?" The elderly ghoul asked, turning off the shredder and stopping it mid-chew. He turned and then froze dead on the spot. His pale brow furrowed, and his sad, dead eyes twinkled with the last remaining dregs of life. At the counter was a face from the past that he thought he'd never see again.

Confused, weary, not believing his bloodshot eyes, the elderly ghoul uttered a name he hadn't said in years:

"Orpheus?"

The elderly ghoul and Orpheus shared the same surprised features as they stared at one another.

Then, Orpheus said the one word that confirmed the suspicion, and surprise turned to cold shock.

"Dad?"

12

Yes, it was Orpheus's father, Apollo Hellenbach, all right. What had happened to him? He was a stooped, drained, pale-faced EBN ghoul. More *compos mentis* than the other drones Orpheus had encountered, but he was a shell of his former self. His sunken eyes were filled with sadness, and his red, bruised lips folded over one another as he slowly walked toward his son.

"How unfortunate to see you," Apollo said.

A thousand things fired through Orpheus's troubled mind. But a slice of understanding cut through them all: this is what happened to his father, where he'd disappeared to; he'd been forced into some kind of soul-sucking servitude to EBN. This had happened to all the other kids' parents his age! Why were there so many orphans in the Grey Zone, like Razoreus and Scratch? Their parents had ended up here in this white-collar nightmare.

Apollo quickly unlatched the counter, lifting it up and allowing Orpheus access. "You better get in here, son." Apollo quickly snapped the counter door shut.

Orpheus inspected the stuffy space filled with shredded files where his father dwelled. "What are you doing here?"

His father shrugged. "Working for the network, son. We shred the memory files of the new arrivals before they go upriver to PTR."

Orpheus smiled with disbelief. "What?"

"When people come here, they get shredded so that when they get reborn again, they don't remember anything about their past lives. It's kind of sad to get reborn, go out, and make the same mistakes all over." Apollo shrugged. "What can I tell you? The system sucks."

Those were the files that were handed to him at reception: Orpheus's life. His memories, his existence, and it was his father's job to destroy them all.

"How'd you get involved in all this?" Orpheus asked.

"Unwillingly drafted. It has its perks. Some of us had the good fortune to become members of the club. Your mother and I, before we can retire to the Elysium Fields Golf and Country Club, we have to put in some time for the network. Well... son, give me your papers."

Apollo went to grab his son's documentation printed at the EBN reception desk, but Orpheus wouldn't let go.

"Hold on," Orpheus said, shaking his head. "I'm not dead."

Apollo laughed. "You were always so impetuous. Look on the positive side; you're better off not having a memory around here. Remembering around here only makes it worse."

A foul feeling rippled through Orpheus. EBN hadn't taken his father's memory. Instantly, he identified Orpheus as his son. Maybe his father hadn't been taken and forced to work here. Maybe his father had given up — given up on him — with the promise of a better life in the future. The Elysium Fields Golf and Country Club. What a crock.

Apollo tried to grab Orpheus's documentation, and again, Orpheus pulled it away.

"Wait a minute. I just got married. I'm not supposed to be here, and neither is my wife."

Apollo nodded, seemed to understand, and then grabbed Orpheus's documentation and tried to feed it through the shredder. "Don't worry, this won't hurt."

Orpheus fought back, trying to pull his documentation back from his treacherous father.

A female voice burst from behind Orpheus: "What is this?"

Orpheus and his father stopped fighting, and both turned in the voice's direction. Orpheus's eyes almost bulged from his skull as he whispered, "*Mother.*"

There was a pause as recognition spread over the female pale-faced ghoul's face.

"Orpheus!"

Yes, it was his mother: Calliope Hellenbach. She too had gone under the un-dead transformation that his father had, but she still had warmth in her bloodshot eyes. Calliope ran across the data-shredded room and threw herself into her son's arms.

"Mother, don't let Dad shred my memory."

"What?" Calliope gasped.

"I just came here to find my wife. We just got married."

"Oh dear," Orpheus's mother said, pulling away from her son. "That's terrible. Who is the lucky girl?"

Orpheus took a deep, sorrowful breath. "Her name is Eurydice."

Orpheus's mother straightened the lapel of her son's neon pink leopard print jacket.

"Oh dear," his mother said again sadly. "Well, unfortunately, everyone who comes here has to let go of their memory."

Orpheus's father interrupted. "If we were to let you go free and you get caught, your mother and I would be subjected to a hundred thousand years of word processing. Do you want to put your mother through that type of hell?"

Orpheus held his head low. What was happening? Today was supposed to be the best day of his life. Now, it was an upside-down nightmare. He wanted to have his parents with him on his wedding day, but not like this.

His father snorted in annoyance. "This Eurydice, she's only a dream."

"A dream!" Orpheus snapped.

"That's right!" his father snapped back. "Just something too good to be true."

"That's why I need to find her," Orpheus said.

His father shook his head. "You'll always be the same,

Orpheus. Always trying to buck the system."

His mother playfully nudged his father, "Where do you think he learned that?"

A little life flushed his father's face.

"Look, I'm just trying to find Eurydice. If you know where she is, help me," Orpheus pleaded.

A smile broke on his mother's cold grey face. "What if we selectively shred the papers that deal with his memory of us?" she asked Apollo. "If he has no memory of us, they can't trace it."

A pained expression crossed Apollo's face as he shifted away with an, "Eh."

A loud pounding came from the door.

"Hurry it up in there!"

It was another EBN employee.

Trouble.

"Hold on," Apollo called back. "We're trying to fix the feeder!"

Orpheus and Calliope became worried. Orpheus looked around the room to see if there was another way out, but there was nothing.

"All right," Apollo said to his wife. "Give me the papers, and for God's sake Orpheus, don't be careless out there."

Reluctantly, Orpheus gave his father the papers. He could feel the transference in power, handing a physical representation of his essence to the man who had disappeared from his life. Could he be trusted? Orpheus could only hope. He looked into his mother's tired, bloodshot eyes and hugged her tightly.

Apollo shook Orpheus's hand as they hugged. "Goodbye, son." He walked to the shredder, flipping through the file of Orpheus's life, plucking free any pages connected to Calliope and himself being the man's parents.

The second the pages touched the Shredder's biting blades, an odd glow enveloped Orpheus. His head vibrated from the inside out as a probing finger penetrated his brain and started to scratch the memories of his parents away. Moments, conversations, good times, bad times, and even the images of their faces were erased from existence. Then, any remnant of them in Orpheus's past was gone. Orpheus jolted out of his mother's arms, disoriented, looking left and right as if he'd been beamed down.

Apollo walked up to him, rolled the files of his son's life gently, and slid them into the inside pocket of Orpheus's jacket.

"Oh, excuse me," Orpheus said awkwardly. "I'm looking for a woman. Her name's Eurydice, she's a dancer."

Apollo and Calliope looked at one another. It had worked. Their son was gone.

"Dancer, huh?" said Apollo. "Try the hall on your right — last door."

Orpheus nodded, ready to track down his love.

"Eh, do I know you?" Apollo asked, grabbing Orpheus's arm as he tried to leave, just checking.

"No," Orpheus said simply. He turned away from the two strangers before him and threw the room's door open, not even looking at the EBN employee on the other side, as he continued his mission to find Eurydice.

Apollo and Calliope watched the man who used to be their son leave, and sadness

sunk into their miserable features.

"No, you don't know us, son," Apollo said, tears building in his bloodshot eyes. "No, you don't."

13

On the *Praise The Ray* soundstage of the EBN building, a huge neon purple eye sizzled on a backdrop of extreme green and silver slashes. All three video cameras were live with the figure in the stage's spotlight, the Hi-Def Dracula and EBN head honcho, Hades Hecata. He had a sly, smug grin, knowing that his image was broadcast into the homes of thousands of potential victims, whose souls he'd lull through the waves of the screen that night. He swayed softly from side to side with mind-numbing Muzak playing as a backing track, and lifted a microphone to his lips, to croon drearily along to camera two.

> *"Up a lazy river by the old mill run.*
> *The lazy, lazy river in the noonday sun.*
> *Linger in the shade of a kind old tree.*
> *Throw away your troubles,*
> *dream a dream with me."*

The studio audience — they couldn't be called *live*; most of them looked dead — all watched Hades' performance from the stand with drab, comatose eyes.

The music did exactly what it was supposed to do: suppress any signs of excitement or stimulus.

But in the hallways leading down to the sound stage, the mundane music had an adverse effect. The performance piped through the building's PA system as Orpheus plowed up a steep flight of stairs, ankle-deep with shredded data files. Anger over Eurydice pushed him on. He found himself going slower with each step.

What was happening?

As Orpheus descended, the shredded data files became knee-deep. Dot-matrix ribbons flapped about his feet. He pushed on, sweating, frustration fueling him as the shredded data reached waist height; he felt like he was trying to plow through a thick snowdrift.

Disrupting the destroyed data as he lurched through it made giant tumbleweeds of shredded paper roll down the steep stairs, crashing into him from behind and rolling down to the ground floor. Orpheus tried to shield the Lyre-Axe — tried to shield himself — as more and more chunks of balled-up paper plummeted past him. He clenched his teeth, kept his head down and pressed on, as Hades' shitty song echoed out around him.

> *"Blue skies up above,*
> *everyone's in love.*
> *Up a lazy river,*
> *how happy you could be.*
> *Up a lazy river with meeeeee!"*

Hades played a sickening solo on an electronic recorder, making Orpheus even angrier. He had to find Eurydice, get her out of this uninteresting environment, and return to the Grey Zone. Compared to this place, the Grey Zone was a cornucopia of culture.

As the miserable Muzak ended, Orpheus reached the bottom of the stairwell. The sign on the door in front of him said: *Praise The Ray: Main Studio*. It was time to go to work. Get in, find Eurydice, and get out. Orpheus ripped through the last ribbons of shredded data, grabbed the door handle, and rushed inside.

Orpheus staggered to a stop on the other side of the door, slamming it shut behind him. The hallway he stood in now had a little more life than the rest of the EBN building, but not much. Instead of grey walls, they were a putrid pea green, with turd brown carpets. Orpheus froze on the spot as a familiar, but not friendly, face walked up to a door ahead; it was the Video Vampire from the Thrash Bin Club. He should have knocked his block off when he had the chance.

The Video Vampire opened the door and called into the room: "Okay. Fiberglass Performance Ensemble. Ten minutes."

From the room, a group of EBN grey-faced ghouls all walked out in perfect precision, smallest to tallest, in drab dark clothes, making their way towards *Praise The Ray*'s main soundstage. The Video Vampire turned to Orpheus, thinking he was another act for tonight's entertainment, trying to cut the line to get some TV time. Then a bulb went off inside his head; he recognized this guy and understood why he was here. He's not such a big man now that his files have been shredded.

The Video Vampire stormed towards Orpheus. "Hey, man. What's your trip?"

"I'm trying to find someone," Orpheus replied.

"Well, that's very nice to know," the Video Vampire replied. "But what are you going to do on stage?"

"I'm not going to do anything on stage," Orpheus

laughed disbelievingly. "I'm just trying to find Eurydice."

Agitation flashed over the Video Vampire's face. No one asks questions; no one who gets down to the production levels does so without getting their memory shredded. How the hell did this guy get here? Those ghouls in processing were slipping. This could mean trouble.

"I don't know who you're talking about, but if you're not in the show, you're not supposed to be here."

"Look, I'm just trying to find my wife. I was told she was down here. She's a dancer."

"Hey, I don't care who she is," the Video Vampire interrupted, "I think you better go now."

The Video Vampire poked his index fingers into Orpheus as if shooing off a stray dog. Orpheus's instinct was to snap them off, but a cooing voice came from behind the Video Vampire.

"*Woo-hoo*, Mr. Producer!" a hand gripped the Video Vampire's shoulder. For a second, Orpheus thought it looked like the claw of a carrion bird.

"Just one moment, please!"

There in a shiny blue dress was Persephone Hecata. Her voice was soft and silky, but there wasn't an octave that felt trustworthy. She eyed Orpheus up and down, liking what she saw. "It's clear you're not supposed to be here, but you are a musician, are you not?"

"Yeah," Orpheus replied.

"Well, if you wish to stay, why don't you play?"

The Video Vampire didn't like being overruled, but Persephone was one half — along with Hades — of the owners of *Praise The Ray*. "Okay, Sparky, what's it going to
be?"

Orpheus had to stay in the building to find Eurydice, even if it meant playing along with their little fantasy. He had a job to do. He held the Lyre-Axe up to the Video Vampire and Persephone, switching it on so its faceplate glowed; a feedback hum came from the mini electronic interface system.

The Video Vampire hung his head and nodded. It was a bad idea to keep someone down here with an unshredded memory. But he could see that devious twinkle in Persephone's eyes. Who was he to go against her will?

Persephone grinned at Orpheus with her tombstone teeth, eyes narrowing like a lizard. A cold shiver bolted down Orpheus's spine.

I'm gonna play, and I'm gonna stay, all right. Then I'm getting my wife out of this hellhole.

> He determined also the dark underworld
> should recognize the misery of death,
> he dared descend by the Taenarian gate
> down to the gloomy Styx. And there passed
> through pale-glimmering phantoms, and the
>   ghosts
> escaped from sepulchers, until he found
> Persephone and Pluto, master-king
> of shadow realms below: and then began
> to strike his tuneful lyre,
> to which he sang.

14

"*Laaaaa! La! La! La! La!*" were the only lyrics of the song sung by the awful a cappella group, the Fiberglass Performance Ensemble, currently on *Praise The Ray*'s stage. They were a zombie gospel choir whose lone musical talent was to drone out the same sound over and over. "*La! La! La!! La!! La!*" straight into the live mic to be broadcast over the airwaves, keeping the viewers nice and docile. As soon as EBN was finished with them, ghouls would zip them back up into the body bags return them to cold storage for later use. Of course, the "live," undead studio audience was hardly the most discerning of crowds. They, too, were thawed-out corpses from the same freezers; shells with enough cognizance to keep their eyes open and clap when prompted.

Hades watched from his black leather throne. Persephone was seated on her own throne beside him. Hades was genuinely impressed by the triteness of the Fiberglass Performance Ensemble. This kind of non-entertainment would keep his audience asleep so slipping their souls through a screen would be nice and easy.

Persephone watched on, bored as usual. She was

tired of all the hackneyed performances she was forced to watch on the *Praise The Ray* stage. The same-old same-old went over with pale-faced ghouls, but for anyone with two chromosomes to rub together, it became tedious fast.

The Fiberglass Performance Ensemble continued to croon: "*Blahhhh! Blah! Blah! Blah! Blah!*"

This is why Persephone let Orpheus stay. Maybe setting a little fire would spice things up. A sly grin passed her lips; she hoped the studio cameras didn't catch it.

With one long "*Blahhhhhhhhhh!*" the Fiberglass Performance Ensemble finished, and Hades and Persephone limply clapped for the lame excuse for entertainment.

"Praise The Ray!" Hades said into camera two, then he turned to the poor example of a band next to him. "Thank you very much. That was completely dull."

No one would argue with that.

Hades looked directly into camera two, now zoomed in for a close-up. "My fellow vapors, we will continue with more on the Euthanasia Network after these messages."

The EBN feed cut to commercial. The camera was zoomed tight to a small TV set with the EBN neon eye logo. A voiceover stated: "Lou, from the Euthanasia Network PTR, presents…" The camera pulled out to reveal a cheesy-looking guy with a fixed smile and cheap gameshow host clothes pointing to the small TV "The traveling ray!" the man exclaimed.

To the side of the stage, Orpheus watched the commercial on a monitor and shivered. The traveling ray… It wasn't enough they wanted to get you ad-dicted to TV at home, now they wanted your atten-tion on the move, twenty-four hours a day, seven days a week. With EBN, the reality through a glass tube was more real than reality itself, and you would never escape it if they had their way.

"Now, brothers and sisters," the cheesy salesman said, "you can take the microwave gospel wherever you go; to work, to school, even on vacation. And eventually, friends, it will save you thousands of dollars because the more you watch, the less you move. The traveling ray comes complete with EBN batteries and a handy carrying case. Friends, don't live a day without the ray!"

The salesman turned the tiny screen to face him. It over-exaggerated him as the TV's radiation glowed over his face like an artificial sun. "Boy!" he grinned. "That does feel good! Order now! Our toll-free operators are standing by."

Orpheus plucked the strings of the Lyre-Axe. Maybe this was meant to be. Maybe he was in this place for a reason. He hated all this banal EBN bullshit like everyone in the Grey Zone. Maybe it was fate he was here with the Lyre-Axe, mistaken as one of their acts, pushed to perform by Persephone.

"Okay, let's get you set up." The Video Vampire was looking over his shoulder, his headphones and mic on as he organized the show.

Orpheus looked out at the lights and cameras on the *Praise The Ray* stage.

If they wanted a performance, he'd give them one, all right.

Orpheus was frog-marched to the center stage by the Video Vampire as Hades watched on with contemptuous eyes. Whoever this new act was, Hades didn't think he was going to give them an EBN-approved performance. Persephone whispered to Hades, and a slimy grin spread over the *Praise The Ray* host's face.

There was a cue that they were coming back from commercial, and Hades straightened, looking into camera two. "Our next performance is for a very special guest. He has just arrived from the other side of our microwaves to perform on a Gibsonian Lyre-Axe. Please welcome Orpheus."

Hades and Persephone clapped limply at Orpheus.

A dead silence came from the un-dead crowd, a stark difference from the rowdy rockers at the Thrash Bin Club.

Orpheus clicked on the Lyre-Axe. Its faceplate lit up; the dull feedback sound ran to the mini electronic interface system on his left wrist. He clicked a button on the interface, and the lifeless studio filled with a booming electronic backbeat. Orpheus began to rock to the beat, grooving to the jam, and started to pluck the Lyre-Axe's strings, stretching out chords straight from the seventies that would make Jimi rock in his grave.

The space around Orpheus warped and twisted, the Lyre-Axe bending light and the perception of reality in some psychedelic way, making the un-dead studio audience twitch in their seats. This was music. It had a heart, a soul, and a rhythm, unlike anything that had been processed through EBN's microwaves before. The audience reacted in a way they had never been intended to; they acknowledged each other, silently agreeing with Orpheus's tunes. Heads started to bang, toes started to tap, and hands started to pad along with the beat.

Disgust rushed over Hades' face; nothing broadcast by EBN was supposed to be enjoyed!

Orpheus playing became a blurring maelstrom of color and light. His music became louder and louder like a heartbeat, giving life where there was only stagnant death. The audience went crazy, rocking, reeling out, head banging, moshing, going nuts! Usually, limp limbs flailed left and right, un-dead bodies filled with a life they had long forgotten. Orpheus's music through the Lyre-Axe was a shot of life to EBN's rays, like a shot of battery acid into a vein. Everyone was alert, awake, *alive*! Tingling and twitching and dancing.

"It's art, dear," Persephone said to Hades with a shrug. Hades gave her a foul look back and clenched his fist tight. This wasn't what *Praise The Ray* was about. *Praise The Ray* was about creating a passive addiction to the underwhelming, not enjoying what was broadcast! He looked around the studio, giving a thumb to everyone behind the scenes, telling them to jerk this guy off stage like they had a huge cane with a hook on the end. No one noticed; they were all too absorbed in Orpheus's performance. Hades exited his throne and marched towards the show's producer.

The Video Vampire was transfixed, watching the live monitor as Orpheus's light-bending performance shifted off-screen in almost the same way as the drudgery sucked people in. Lights and color warped outwards, infecting reality with something more than the soul-sucking status quo of their station. Hades wrenched the headset from the Video Vampire and snapped into the mic:

"Master control, fade to black. *Now!*"

Orpheus's image immediately faded to a pinprick of light on the monitor.

"Superimpose maximum hypno-pulse and cut to commercial. *Now!*"

The EBN neon eye appeared on the screen.

Hades grabbed the Video Vampire by the lapels. "No doubt we are losing thousands of viewers every second! Go on, go!"

Hades threw the Video Vampire aside, ran to Orpheus, and stopped him from playing. Hades clenched his fist, pulled Orpheus off-stage.

Who does this mortal think he is to try and take over my station?

It was time to teach the invader of his airwaves a lesson.

This was going to be fun.

15

"We work eternal hours *sedating*," Hades snapped at Orpheus. "What kind of stunt are you trying to pull?"

"I'm not trying to pull anything!" Orpheus said.

"Oh, come on, dear," Persephone begged. "Would you please lighten up?"

"How did you get in here?" Hades demanded.

"I don't know," Orpheus said genuinely. "I came here because I'm looking for Eurydice. I was told I could find her here."

Behind Orpheus, the Video Vampire cracked his neck and sneered.

"Well," Hades said with a grin, "isn't that the pits? Her being here, and for that matter, you being here. It is inevitable, so why fight it?"

"Why don't you let us out of here?" Orpheus demanded

Hades tried to keep composed, but the anger in him flared. "So, you want to intervene with destiny? I don't think so!"

Persephone interrupted. "Dear, would you please come here for a moment?" She pushed Hades back into the shadows behind the *Praise The Ray* stage.

74

"Why are you being such a hard ass?" she asked. "This is love and devotion."

Hades sighed with annoyance.

"You can make any rule you want. So why don't you have a little charity?"

Hades laughed. "Charity? Are you serious?"

Persephone nodded. "Yes. You let me go on summer vacations."

Hades shook his head slightly. "Dear, you are too avant-garde. First, you want this guy to play, and now you want him to leave this woman?"

Persephone cracked what almost looked like a genuine smile as she looked at Orpheus. "Just this once."

Hades brought his right index finger up to Persephone's lips to silence her. "Okay, but they won't have carte blanche."

Persephone pulled away from Hades' touch; Hades stormed over to Orpheus and stood before him, toe-to-toe.

"Well, sonny boy, this is your lucky day. You know you've been such a pain in the ray, but Persephone seems to feel you and your wife deserve a chance to live. So, you may leave."

A brief wave of relief washed over Orpheus.

"But there is one condition," Hades smirked.

"Hades, we're on in ten seconds," the Video Vampire informed him. "We better get back on stage."

Hades pushed Orpheus back into the center of the *Praise The Ray* stage. The undead audience just stared at them with vacant eyes.

"You okay?" Hades asked Orpheus.

"Yeah," Orpheus replied.

The Video Vampire counted them in from five.

Four.

Three.

Two.

He pointed at Hades; they were live on the air. The low drone of the *Praise The Ray* ident began to play.

"Welcome back! With that obnoxious performance, Orpheus has qualified to play our new PTR game: *Don't Look Back.* The contestant may leave the Euthanasia Network with his bride if he can do it without looking back at her."

Orpheus gave Hades a look.

What was he saying?

"If he succeeds, it's an all-expense paid honeymoon vacation to the Grey Zone for two!"

The live feed cut to camera three, where Persephone modeled a TV monitor, seductively touching its plastic sides as an image of the shipping container slums of the Grey Zone shows on its screen. Hades clapped as, behind the scenes, the video control room piped in cheers to the soundtrack.

"Are you ready to play?"

"You bet," Orpheus answered. There was something supernaturally serpentine about EBN's practices, but how could they uphold something as trivial as *Don't Look Back*?

"As you leave," Hades said, "Eurydice will follow behind you, but you must never look back at her until you have *both* completed your exit. Understand?"

Orpheus swallowed hard and nodded. A part of him thought this was all performance madness, but another part understood EBN couldn't be trusted. How could they keep Eurydice away from him if he didn't play the game and decided to look back at his love? He didn't want to find out.

"And remember," Hades told him sincerely, "don't look back."

Hades lit a cigarette and blew smoke into the air.

Orpheus gripped the Lyre-Axe tight and said again, "You bet."

The game was about to begin.

* * *

Praise The Ray cut to a handheld camera in a hallway outside the soundstage where the Video Vampire led Orpheus along. The Video Vampire stopped and spun around to face him, sneering, "You are one lucky sucker."

"Gee, thanks a lot," Orpheus said, holding in his rage.

There was a shuffling noise behind Orpheus, and he started to turn. Quickly, he sharpened his senses.

Don't look back! Don't look back!

"Is she there?" Orpheus asked the grinning Video Vampire.

"Why don't you turn around and find out?"

"Very funny," Orpheus replied.

Behind him, two EBN ghouls unzipped Eurydice from an EBN-branded body bag and helped her to her feet. She was dazed and confused from her fall off the car lot's roof, but she pushed aside the pain until she and Orpheus escaped.

"Eurydice, are you there?" Orpheus asked.

She staggered, bumped into Orpheus, and he heard her hollow voice: "I'm here."

"Let's go," Orpheus demanded as the Video Vampire signaled the handheld cameraman to come down next to him for a close-up of Orpheus's face.

The Video Vampire opened a door at the end of the hall, and the cameraman backed out into the stairwell of destroyed data bails lining the floor. Orpheus followed him, Eurydice behind, with the Video Vampire at the rear of the pack as they ascended.

Orpheus could hear his heart thump in his ears as he stepped forward, one foot after the other, in the piles of shredded dot-matrix data. He had to be careful; he couldn't fall backward and look up at Eurydice, or it would all be over. It was a straightforward thing: don't look back.

But running through his mind were all the ways that this might go wrong. What if he saw her in the reflection of a camera lens pointed in his face? What about glass windows? Would the bastards consider that looking back? He couldn't risk it. He fixed his gaze forward.

The Video Vampire stopped and watched them go, hissing, "See you *sooonnnn*…"

Orpheus staggered forward, his feet tangled in the ribbons of shredded memories on the stairs as they ascended. Eurydice stumbled and almost fell into him. She felt woozy, tired, awful, but this was the final furlong to freedom.

Hades and Persephone watched all this on live feedback in the *Praise The Ray* studio.

The handheld cameraman stood to one side, allowing Orpheus and Eurydice to pass. Orpheus shivered. Was the cameraman going to trip him so he'd turn and fall? Worry melted over Orpheus like hot wax. But the cameraman did nothing. Ahead, a door opened autonomously, and a breeze of cold night air whispered in.

They were nearly outside.

The nightmare was nearly over.

Orpheus reached out and pushed the door open further. There was a small crowd from his wedding outside: Axel, Razoreus, Scratch, Linus. All his friends. Orpheus was free, out of the EBN building. They had made it.

Relief passed each of their faces as Orpheus walked towards them.

Then Scratch looked past Orpheus and cried in delight, "Eurydice!"

Elated, thinking Eurydice was right behind him back on the streets of the Grey Zone, Orpheus turned around to face his love.

But Eurydice wasn't out of the building.

She was still standing on the doorjamb. As their eyes met, Orpheus gasped. Eurydice disappeared from existence as if she'd never even been there, gone as fast as someone snapping their fingers, and the door to the EBN building banged shut. Orpheus ran to the door, grabbed the handle, and flung it open finding... bricks. No entrance, no doorway, no way in or out of the building.

Nothing.

Orpheus had lost.

How could they take her? How could they do this?

Orpheus punched the brick wall until his knuckles bled.

Then he slumped against it in despair. A hollow carved-out feeling gored through his belly.

That was it.

It was over.

Orpheus was alone.

He had to follow one rule.

Don't look back.

He looked back.

Eurydice was gone.

And so was his hope that his life would be any more than just a dull ripple in the dull Grey Zone.

After that, nothing mattered.

Eurydice... no...

79

AN OVIDEO FOR THE MASSES...
AN UPDATE...

> Orpheus implored in vain the ferry man
> to help him cross the River Styx again,
> but was denied
> the very hope of death.

MESSAGE CONCLUDED.

The screens were never dead, but had nothing significant to say for months and months. Then one night, Ovideo bloomed again in the dark and sought its dormant quarry:

> *Dying the second time, she could not say*
> *a word of censure of her husband's fault;*
> *what had she to complain*
> *of his great love?*
> *Her last word spoken was,*
> *"Farewell!"*
> *which he could barely hear,*
> *and with no further sound*
> *she fell from him again*
> *to Hades.*

16

One year later.

It was all a big setup. Even if Scratch hadn't blown it by yelling at Orpheus, these Euthanasia people knew what they were doing. After the disaster at the wedding and his performance on *Praise The Ray*, Orpheus became kind of famous in the Zone. He didn't give a shit, and his friends hardly ever saw him.

But occasionally, they would get him out for a cruise in a garage called Devo. It was a thirteen-story parking lot, a stack of cracked concrete slabs that was always empty at night. Axel, Razoreus, Scratch, and a couple of other Zoners met on the thirteenth floor. They stood looking out at the night; the sound of rumbling skateboard wheels echoed around the space.

Orpheus skidded up on his deck, dressed in black so he could fade into the shadows if there was trouble. One of the Zoners brought a boombox, plugged in a tape, hit play, and ripped out a neo-punk tune. The lead singer's voice reverberated around them:

"I don't know what to do!

I don't know what to say!
You don't know what to do!
You don't know what to say!"

Razoreus banged his head as the group lined up. Scratch looked up and down the motley crew of Zoners finished lining up, then rasped out, "Okay, let's go!"

They kicked off on their decks, downhill skating as fast as possible, picking up speed on the parking lot's down ramps. Concrete pillars flew past them as the wind cut against exposed flesh like a blade. Axel lay flat on his board, dead legs stretched before him, punching the floor with his welding gloves to keep speed. He shifted his body to maneuver the corners and kept pace with the able-bodied boarders around him.

The strip lights overhead fluttered and buzzed like insects as they thrashed beneath them, dipping in and out of shadow. They cruised tight corners winding to the ground floor, wheels clattering and grinding as they rolled. They were a group of sidewalk surfers grinding out a sketchy landscape.

Orpheus kicked the ground, picking up speed, going faster and faster. The speed helped with the pain and distracted him from everything he had lost along with Eurydice. People asked around after she disappeared, but EBN denied all knowledge. They said it was all part of the show.

It wasn't like he could go to the cops; they had been decommissioned years ago, thanks to EBN's promise of keeping the populace docile. Crime was down 95% thanks to the brainwashing with RF microwave frequencies. EBN could do what they wanted when they wanted, and anyone who challenged that was fucked.

David Irons

Orpheus cut the night he lost Eurydice up in his mind in so many ways that the whole scenario was memory confetti. There were too many what-ifs: what if he had just gone in all guns blazing and nailed Hades and that Video Vampire? What if he had just grabbed Eurydice and run for the door? What if he had never looked back? He would never know because none of that had happened. He had looked back, and all he could do now was regard Eurydice in the past tense.

His lost love.

Gone.

Where the hell was she? The more he had thought about being in that EBN building on the *Praise The Ray* soundstage, the more he understood exactly where that place was: Hell. They knew weird shit went down in that EBN building. But being in there, up close to Hades and Persephone Hecata, there was something devilish about the pair.

Orpheus had been so caught up in the past that he'd taken a turn too tight, misjudged his angle, bailed, and slammed into one of the Devo's concrete walls. Both his feet came off the ground, and he twisted and slammed on the ground. Total wipeout. Orpheus let out a grunt and enjoyed the pain. The pain was good. He was glad he never wore a brain bucket. The pain was a distraction from all the gloom in his head. Maybe if he cracked his cranium open, all the awful stuff inside would leak out. Eurydice gave life a glow. Now, an inescapable darkness shadowed everything.

Scratch, who was a beat behind Orpheus and watched the wreck, skidded to a stop and exclaimed, "Radical!"

Razoreus and Scratch picked Orpheus up, dusted him down, and put him back on his deck. Razoreus kicked off, skating after the others as they thrashed to the ground floor. He yelled, "Come on!" and beckoned Scratch and Orpheus to keep going. They both did, skillfully catching up with Axel and the other Zoners, making it down to the ground floor and pushing off into the night. It was a successful sesh, but the grinding had just begun. Orpheus's bell was still ringing from the stack. Maybe, if more thoughts of the past — when he was happy — entered his head, he'd try and eradicate them with another burnout. Maybe break something that wouldn't heal to keep him on edge.

That had already happened, though.

Eurydice's disappearance had broken his heart.

* * *

After the other Zoners left the group, Axel, Scratch, Razoreus, and Orpheus all skated into the night. It should have been like old times; Orpheus was there in body, but he wasn't there in spirit. He was haunted by the past, slowly spiraling into a distant misery. There was melancholy being together like this, holding onto the scraps of a good time, just hanging out and pretending everything was normal. Having a few laughs on their decks. It was transient and fleeting, what they had right now wouldn't last, but no one said it out loud. Things would change because Orpheus was changing, a victim to his own grief with no way to escape the sadness in his soul. Little distractions like the excursion tonight helped.

They skated around the desolate sidewalks of the Grey Zone, heading out into the derelict industrial area. An odd glow came from a half-open roller shutter door leading to an underground parking lot to the EBN building. Orpheus skated toward it.

He skidded to a stop before it, and a chill ran up his spine. What the hell was in there? Why was it so clammy and cold being near it? A blue neon hue escaped under the metal door, entwining with a ghostly vapor. A sulfurous stink lingered in the air. Another feeling, like someone walking over his grave, shuddered through Orpheus's body as he bent down and stared at the eerie void. The others all ground their decks to a stop next to him.

"Hey, let's check this one out," Orpheus suggested.

"You're not going in there," Scratch told him, grabbing Orpheus and pulling him away.

"Why not?" Orpheus replied. A morbid curiosity wrapped around Orpheus like a slimy tentacle. He needed to know what the hell was in that parking lot.

"It's not cool. It's not rad," Scratch replied, trying to find the right words. "It's the pits, man."

"What do you mean?"

"Guys who have tried to escape this garage never get past the security."

"The security!"

Scratch didn't know it, but they were only making things worse. The odd underground parking lot suddenly became Pandora's Box in Orpheus's head. He needed to know what was—

A hand suddenly grabbed his pants and tugged on them. Orpheus snapped around and looked down, and Axel looked up at him with seriousness. "Even if they get past the security, nobody ever sees them again."

Orpheus's eyes sparkled at the challenge. What was this uncanny urban legend he'd never heard of? "I want to check it out."

He went to turn away from Axel, but the legless

man reached up, nearly falling from his deck, clamping onto Orpheus's arm.

"Hey! Don't be a jerk! That garage is the stairway to hell! It's a hamburger inferno! It's the final thrash! It's a goddamn piece of shit!" Axel yanked Orpheus down to his level and began to wrestle him, repeating, "It's a piece of shit! It's a piece of shit!"

Scratch jumped between them, breaking it up. "Take it easy! Come on, take a blow. Do us all a favor, and don't get him started."

Orpheus scrambled up, grabbed his deck, and stared into the mysterious space beyond the garage door. "Look, I just want to check it out!"

Scratch threw their deck to the ground in rage and pushed Orpheus backward. None of them had ever seen Scratch like this before. Scratch had an easygoing attitude; life was hanging free and making music. But a sudden seriousness possessed Scratch.

"Where do you think I got this?" Scratch said, lifting the bandana around their neck, revealing a badly healed twisted vortex of a scar on their throat. None of the others ever wondered why Scratch talked so scratchily; they just accepted it. Who could have guessed someone had tried to tear Scratch's vocal cords out? Razoreus winced and felt bad for his friend.

"Even if you get in there," Axel cried, "you're gonna need a special deck and wheels that can shred it."

"Where can I find that setup?" Orpheus asked.

"Find it?" Axel laughed crazily. "Shit, man. You don't find it. It finds you."

Orpheus threw his deck on the ground, annoyed, and pushed off into the night. The others slowly followed.

David Irons

There was something in that EBN parking lot, under that roller shutter door he needed to see.

Another shudder rattled his bones.

Special deck or not, friends or no friends, he needed to come back and check it out.

The chattering wheels of his deck sounded like the chomping teeth of a skull.

17

"Leon! Leon! Come on, Leon, listen!" Linus bellowed into his telephone. Whereas Orpheus's life had hit the skids with Eurydice's disappearance, Linus had bent the situation to his advantage the way any good, sleazy manager would. Now, he had an office on the edge of the Grey Zone, filled with posters of all the other acts he now managed. He took full credit for Orpheus's popularity, fabricating a story in which he had connections in the EBN building that gave Orpheus his exposure, and every desperate band in the zone had eaten it up and given him forty percent. His bread and butter was Orpheus, though, and every club in the wasteland wanted to book him. Those were the ones who weren't scared.

Orpheus had become a legend for getting in and out of the EBN building alive. Controversy creates cash, and Linus wanted to use it to drain every dime and opportunity. But there was a worry that booking Orpheus might attract unwanted attention from the EBN executives, and the last thing anyone wanted was a horde of ghouls and video vampires crawling all over their club. Linus tried to book a spot at The Condo, an upmarket thrash joint that paid good moolah. But their booker, Leon, had the usual reservations.

"Leon, look," Linus explained, "You can look at 'em, what's it gonna hurt? They used to be called the Shredders. They're now Orpheus and the Shredders."

Linus paused and listened. It was the same old rigadoon when he mentioned Orpheus's name. "Yeah, that's it, same guy that was on the Euthanasia Network last year and lived to tell the tale, okay. And Leon, look, that translates into mystique. Alchemy lesson. Mystique into publicity. Publicity into greenbacks!'

Linus heard a sigh from the small earpiece. "I know they're popular, I know people will come to see 'em, but I don't need any EBN—"

"Leon, you're blowing smoke!" Linus snapped. "That one time at the Thrash Bin Club was an isolated incident. None of those EBN stiffs have been to one of their shows since. I know you don't have a warm-up for Raging Mucus, and they would be terrific in The Condo."

There was a click on the other end, then dead silence. "Don't put me on hold!"

Linus tossed the receiver onto his desk. Booking Orpheus and the Shredders had been hard lately. Not just because of EBN baggage but also because of Orpheus's attitude. Linus couldn't blame the guy; losing a diamond like Eurydice was like losing a briefcase stuffed with a million dollars. But you had to keep going, roll with life's punches, and turn a negative into a positive. Orpheus let the past get on top of him and pollute the present. He couldn't say Orpheus was depressed, but shortness and anger ate away at the edges of his personality. He'd pissed off some of the club owners and blown a few opportunities with recording labels when he was hot off *Praise*

The Ray. Linus didn't want to blame the guy, but... but...

Linus sighed, plucked a cigarette from his desk and pushed it between his lips. He stared into the phone's receiver and said, "I hate your guts," then hung up on Leon.

* * *

Linus had booked Orpheus and the Shredders at the Thrash Bin Club for the Slash and Burn battle of the bands that night. There was a worry about Orpheus turning up — there always seemed to be worries about Orpheus these days. He was thirty minutes late and came bounding on stage, ready to blow down the Thrash Bin's walls.

The club's MC took to the stage and announced, "Get ready, humanoids, the next entry is the Grey Zone's ultimate grinders, Orpheus and the Shredders! Yeah! Let's give them some shit! *Yeah!*" His words riled up the crowd. They screamed and cheered as Orpheus made his way on stage to the center spotlight and grabbed the mic.

"All right, thank you!" Orpheus called to the Thrash Bin's crowd. "Some things just can't be said. They can't be whistled either, but we're gonna play it."

The Shredders' drummer started pounding an aggressive beat as Orpheus ran to one side of the stage, parallel to their rhythm guitarist, who stood on the other side.

Since Orpheus's popularity rose after his EBN exposure, Linus had secured funding to enhance the Shredders' stage show. Orpheus and the rhythm guitarist reached above the stage where giant, oversized guitars hung on bungee cords. Both pulled the guitars down, thrashed out a chord, and let the guitar snap back toward the Thrash Bin's ceiling. The guitars bounced around, distorting and creating feedback.

Their set wasn't just kick-ass music anymore; it had transmogrified into experimental art that the alternative crowd ate up. Punk girls zoned out, and metal maniacs banged their heads as Orpheus and the rhythm guitarist pounded out abstract chords on the bungee guitars, then fired them out across the crowd.

The crowd tried to jump and grab the guitars, hands firing up into the air, trying to pluck them down. The only interference the guitars had was when some Zone drone launched an inflatable sex doll toward them. How the hell did he manage to get that in past security? Orpheus laughed. The song started to pick up speed, gaining adrenaline. Orpheus ran across the stage, grabbed the Lyre-Axe, and ran back to the center spotlight near the microphone stand.

He tried to turn the Lyre-Axe on, but the faceplate only flickered with light; the instrument produced foul feedback through the club that made the drummer wince. The Shredders were getting pretty pissed with Orpheus, and the damn Lyre-Axe was only part of it.

Orpheus refused to come on stage one night when it wouldn't turn on, and Linus had to run around the zone to find an electric tinkerer to make it work again. From the Shredders' point of view, after his fifteen minutes of fame on *Praise The Ray*, an irritable prima donna persona had wrapped around Orpheus and, at times, made him unbearable.

The band wasn't thrilled that they had become Orpheus and the Shredders; they got it for marketing, and it made sense. But they couldn't tell if his attitude stemmed from the grief of losing Eurydice or his ego.

Either way, they wouldn't put up with his shit forever. Orpheus smashed his fist into the Lyre-Axe's side and the instrument flashed to life. He began to play the instrument, and it blurred the reality around Orpheus as he cranked out psychedelic riffs. The crowd went wild. From a distance, the entire performance was so far out, it was almost in orbit. Orpheus and the Shredders had killed it at the Slash and Burn battle of the bands. But, deep down inside, Orpheus felt empty to his core.

Feeding off the crowd's electricity, Orpheus performed one final psychedelic solo with the Lyre-Axe and was the last offstage when the Shredders' set was over. He ran backstage, where the Shredders all sat around their dressing room table, smoking and drinking. Orpheus slumped down beside them and took an open beer. Their bassist grabbed the can back. "Get your own!"

Orpheus shrugged and grabbed another beer.

"When are you going to get that thing fixed again?" the Shredders' drummer said snidely, nodding at the Lyre-Axe.

"Soon," Orpheus replied simply, more interested in his beer.

"Well, I wish you would," the drummer added. "It's screwing us up."

"Probably needed batteries," the bassist laughed.

A voice bellowed down from the stage. *"Muy bueno, muchachos! Muy bueno!"* Linus came running towards them, full of fake enthusiasm. "Thank you!" he cried, hiking a thumb over his shoulder and glaring at the Shredders. "Thank you! Thank you!"

The Shredders got up from the dressing room table, glared back at Linus, and exited to watch the next band perform. Their drummer gave Orpheus a snake-eyed glance as he left.

95

Preferential treatment for the prima donna. Give me a break.

Linus leaned against the wall next to Orpheus and stared at his star. "All right, Orpheus. Better late than never, huh?"

"Right," was Orpheus's cold response.

"Right," Linus mimicked. "Look," Linus said, checking over his shoulder that the Shredders had gone. "I want to talk to you about a real sweetheart of a gig I've got cooking. I have an audition for *you* to play for — get this, *Carcinoma Dance*. Sweetness, huh?"

"Right," Orpheus replied flatly.

"Look," Linus snapped. "Shit, man, I busted my ass to get you this audition. Now, these people are interested. They're up-and-comers with damn good money. It's a chance for you to meet some *tres importante* people. Okay? Jesus."

Orpheus shrugged, sighed, and began to fiddle with the Lyre-Axe's mini electronic interface.

Linus looked Orpheus up and down. He was covered in bruises from his late-night boarding sessions with Scratch, Axel, and Razoreus. "Look, it's a nice alternative to thrashing yourself to death, don't you think?"

Orpheus dropped the electronic interface and put his head in his hands. He was sick of all this shit. Why couldn't Linus just fuck off —?

Linus snatched the interface from the dresser and looked like he was ready to snap it in two. Orpheus stared at his manager with dreary eyes.

"Look, dipwad," Linus growled. "Your ass has been dragging around, and it's getting really boring."

Orpheus snatched the interface back and snarled. "Get outta my trench, man."

"No problem," Linus said calmly, teeth gritted.

"The audition's at the old Showbox Ballroom, Tuesday night at nine."

Orpheus said nothing.

"Orpheus, they're professionals. Don't let me down. Promptly, if you can, please. Tuesday, nine o'clock."

"Tuesday at nine," Orpheus echoed.

Linus, agitated and annoyed, stomped away. "He better not let me down over this one, he better not," he mumbled.

"Right," Orpheus muttered.

Right was the word that made all the questions he couldn't be bothered to answer go away.

It was the opposite of how he felt inside.

Wrong.

18

A beaten-up box truck pulled up behind an old warehouse on the border between the Grey Zone and the upper residential districts. It was late — almost three AM, and the moon covered everything in a cool blue hue.

The truck driver had his orders: deliver cereal to the rear of the Dorsia, so that the entitled assholes had something to chew on for breakfast. What a life. All he had to go home to was a shipping container in the Zone and a pot of yesterday's coffee. The truck driver sighed, clambered out, and went inside the warehouse to find some jackoff to empty his truck. Little did he know, two Zoners were already helping him unload.

Razoreus and Scratch had scoped this place out for the last few weeks and had gotten the delivery pattern down to a tee. The second the truck driver had disappeared inside the warehouse door, Scratch had the truck's roller shutter up and was inside with Razoreus standing outside, keeping watch.

"Hurry up, Scratch!" Razoreus snapped as loud as he dared, looking left and right for any eyes that might be watching them.

"I'm shanking it!" Scratch hissed out. "Give me the blade!"

Razoreus tossed a box cutter to Scratch.

Quickly, Scratch slashed open a taped-up box and turned on a flashlight to explore the contents.

Bingo! Shredded Wheat! Boxes of the stuff!

Scratch reached in, grabbed a box, turned it over, and read the ingredients. "No preservatives, no potassium nitrate, real carbohydrates. What a deal!" This was the real stuff.

Razoreus heard a noise from inside the warehouse and called his friend. "Let's go, dip brain!"

Scratch tossed the cereal back into its box and tossed it out the back of the truck to Razoreus. He staggered, grabbed it, and slammed it down on Scratch's deck. Then Scratch tossed another box, and Razoreus threw it onto his deck. Scratch jumped out of the truck, and the pair ran, wheeling their loot off into the shadows of the Grey Zone, laughing like loons as they went. Another successful episode of snatch and run —wait until the others scoped this!

* * *

Orpheus staggered home from the Thrash Bin Club. He didn't bother waiting around to see the results from the first round of the Slash and Burn battle of the bands. Who gave a shit either way? It didn't mean anything. It wasn't going to bring Eurydice back.

A haze of misery encased Orpheus like a black cloud. Any Zoners who passed him could sense the palpable anger and sadness he emitted. Then, suddenly, his bleak demeanor was broken as a sound pricked his ears. It was the same metallic rhythm Scratch was always banging out.

Orpheus followed the sound and found himself by

a gored-out container that had been turned into a makeshift stage. On it, a group of Zoners were using the detritus and debris of the Zone as musical instruments, creating sophisticated industrialist percussion. Engine blocks were used as a drum kit, busted up pots and pans as additional beats. Old guitars wailed with wiring strung where strings should be. It was Scratch's urban sound but magnified into something bigger and slicker, more elaborate and substantial.

The musicians were all masked in either the modified leather of old car seats, wire mesh, or tire rubber. Old fuel pump hoses were modified on one mask into rubber dreadlocks. They were covered in piping and wiring, looking like they were some bio-mechanical extensions of the instruments they played. It was as if Scratch had started a new genre without even knowing it, and this anarchic sound was the new sound of the Grey Zone, cold but beating out a pulse of life.

Rebelliousness forged in the rust of a landscape of shipping containers. It was the counterculture come to life; the antithesis of the sterile sounds of *Praise The Ray* that poisoned people's minds.

Boarders skated around the container, getting into the vibe of the music as they kick-flipped, ollied, and kick-turned their decks to the music. The music was infectious; Orpheus could admit that. Linus was always bleating about finding that "New sound." This was it, alive and kicking in the depths of the Grey Zone.

A cold night wind caught Orpheus as he stood listening. A chill rattled down his spine. Something inside told him things were going to change. Everything was going to change.

* * *

As Orpheus walked back to his shipping container, a shadowed figure skated from the Grey Zone's dark corners and called:

"Hey, Orpheus!"

Orpheus squinted as the figure shifted into the flickering light of a burning barrel. He smiled; it was Razoreus, barely balancing on his deck with a huge pile of Shredded Wheat in his arms.

"Hey, looks like the skate pirates have scored again."

Razoreus dropped every box of Shredded Wheat except one, which he tossed to Orpheus. "Here."

Orpheus laughed and thanked his friend.

"So, how'd the show go?" Razoreus asked.

Orpheus unlocked his shipping container and leaned against the door. "We peeled some paint off the walls."

"Hey, did you get me that tape?" Eagerness gleamed in Razoreus's eyes; he'd been asking for a tape of the Shredders' music for the past few months. Orpheus always seemed distracted and forgot, but not tonight.

"Just so happens you're in luck," Orpheus said, scratching around in his leather jacket's pockets. He pulled out a cassette tape and tossed it to Razoreus. "Greatest hits. Maximum volume."

"All right! Thanks!" Razoreus replied.

"I'll see you later," Orpheus said before he opened the door of his shipping container and disappeared inside, leaving Razoreus to pick up the dropped Shredded Wheat boxes. Of all his friends, young Razoreus always tried the hardest to make Orpheus's existence a little better.

Razoreus remembered the day of Orpheus's wedding; there was an optimism that life could be worth living seeing his friend so happy. Then it was taken away. Razoreus looked up to Orpheus, but every time he looked into his eyes, life seemed to be worth the opposite of living. He tried to talk to Orpheus about what happened with Eurydice, but Razoreus could never find the words. One day, he hoped Orpheus could find peace in life again.

* * *

Inside the shipping container, Orpheus lay on his bed. The carousel lamp rotated slowly, projecting calming pastels. They didn't soften the container's cold metal walls anymore.

He stared at a black-and-white photo of Eurydice and studied her soft face, staring into her dark eyes. Her memory pulled the strings to his soul. It had been a year, but the pain never lessened; it only intensified.

There was a shock when she disappeared; heartache had wrenched his body. Then, over time, the truth of the matter baked into his bone marrow: Eurydice was gone, and he'd never see her again. And each day that passed, he sunk deeper into despair and depression. The memory of Eurydice's ghost haunted him. What had that EBN scum done with her? Was she still alive, living like one of their un-dead drones? Could he ever find out? They were too big to mess with. Everything felt too big and overwhelming to mess with. Orpheus slumped onto his front, sunk into the bed, and stared at the photo of Eurydice. Slowly, he began to slip away into dream.

* * *

The sunset dipped close to the sea turning it red like lava; Orpheus lay on a sandy beach, listening as waves lapped at the shore. It was a deep, lucid dream;

he could feel every grain of sand under him, and the sun beat down on his back.

Slowly, he stirred, eyes adjusting to the hazy magic-hour sun. A cold breeze ran across his body like tip-toeing fingers, and he turned to look at the shoreline. A statuesque female figure stood there, wrapped in a wispy white dress. She was dipping her toe in the sparkling ocean, kicking the water playfully. Orpheus rose to his feet, heart thumping.

Eurydice often appeared in his dreams; tonight, she was back. He moved toward her and placed a hand on Eurydice's shoulder. Immediately, she turned and embraced him. Orpheus picked her up and spun her around and around and around. He placed her back on the beach and whispered, "I love you."

A jolt of shock sliced Orpheus's expression when he stared into her face. It wasn't Eurydice he'd held; it was a grinning, giggling Persephone Hecata. She pulled away from Orpheus and disappeared into nothingness.

A hand touched Orpheus's shoulder, making him jump. He turned to a distraught Eurydice, who asked: "What does that mean?" Orpheus couldn't answer. His throat tightened, and just like that, his whole body disintegrated into a pile of sand.

Instead of blowing away on the evening breeze, Orpheus reformed onto hard asphalt ground. A burning blue light covered his naked body. Cold and confused, he turned. Then he shivered when he understood where he was: outside the open EBN underground parking lot roller shutter that Axel, Razoreus, and Scratch had warned about.

A clammy coldness emanated from inside, a blue neon hue escaped under the shutter, entwined with a ghostly vapor. A sulfurous stink lingered in the air.

Here it was in his dreams, exactly how it was in reality. An awful aura emitted from the gap beneath the shutter. The ghostly vapor whisked around him, clawed at his throat, reached down into his lungs with frigid, icy fingers, and ripped at his guts.

* * *

Orpheus woke in his bed holding his throat. He could still feel the pain he'd only imagined attacking his innards. Slowly, he caught his breath. Dreams were all he had when the waking day felt like a nightmare. Now, his dreams had been invaded by the bleakness EBN inflicted on him. But with this nightmare, a new inspiration seized him.

Something was behind that old roller shutter in the odd underground parking lot.

The dream wasn't a dream; it was a message.

There was something in there, something to do with Eurydice.

He knew it; he just knew it.

Orpheus looked around his cold, empty container. It was time to find out.

19

Orpheus rolled out into the night on his deck, the Lyre-Axe around his neck. The dream's influence pushed him forward.

He glided around the corner of the derelict parking lot and grounded to a stop outside the open underground parking roller shutter. It was the same as the last time he'd come here, exactly like his dream. The same odd burning blue light escaped from the half-closed shutter, the same feeling of dread oozed from underneath, and the same sulfurous smell came from inside. Reality had become a dream, and then the dream had become reality again. They felt oddly the same.

Axel's words rattled his mind: "That garage is the stairway to hell! It's a hamburger inferno!"

Orpheus ducked down and inspected the parking lot's innards. He couldn't see a thing, only the ever-rolling mist filled with blue neon that looked as if it went on forever, an endless sea of curdling mists. A thalassophobic feeling drilled into his mind and rippled through his body. What was he thinking coming here?

Eurydice.

Orpheus said fuck it to fear, dropped belly first on his deck, and pushed himself under the roller shutter, straight into the mysteries beyond.

He rolled straight forward, his only view the shifting mists washing past him until they started to clear. A graffiti-riddled elevator shaft appeared before him. Its red spray-painted door was tagged with obscenities and initials. Only the dripping yellow-and-red text beside the door stood out to him: "RISK IT AND DIE."

Orpheus staggered up, heart thumping as he looked around the otherworldly parking lot. He kick-flipped his deck, caught it, and swiftly moved to the elevator. He pressed the elevator's call button, and the red spray-painted door instantly peeled open. Orpheus quickly stepped inside, and the door automatically slid shut as the elevator moved downwards.

His heart started to thump fast, and trepidation tightened around his neck like a noose. The elevator's mechanisms moaned as it started to shift. Axel's mad words haunted his head. *"It's the final thrash! It's a god-damn piece of shit!"*

The elevator swayed slightly; a whine came from its cable like a soul escaping hell.

Nothing felt good about what he was doing.

He looked up. Above him, hanging in the elevator's corner like a one-eyed metal bat was an EBN camera — just the same as the ones he'd stared into in the EBN building the night Eurydice disappeared.

It figures those fuckers would have something to do with this macabre, strange setup. He stared into the dead eye of the camera lens. Which one of the goon squad was watching—?

Suddenly, the elevator door was wrenched open, and a huge hand shot through and started to strangle Orpheus. Orpheus kicked and struggled, taken by surprise at the attack. He tried to fight back, but his assailant's strength was overpowering. He was slammed backward into the elevator wall, gasping for air as the hand squeezed his windpipe.

He hadn't even heard the elevator stop or felt it jar to a standstill on a floor, but before him was the biggest, ugliest grey-faced EBN ghoul he'd ever seen. His face was all grimaced teeth, evil squinting eyes, and cords popping from his neck as he squeezed tighter and tighter. Orpheus gasped and tried to fight back, but every blow he dealt on the oversized bastard did nothing.

A frightening idea flashed in Orpheus's mind. Scratch's ravaged voice rasped: "Where do you think I got this?" Then he saw an image of the twisted vortex of a scar on Scratch's throat. Was this the EBN goon that ruined his friend's vocal cords? As the oversized ghoul's fingernails sunk into his flesh, he understood the answer. Spittle flew from Orpheus's lips as he gasped for air; in a second, there would be no more Orpheus and the Shredders, just the Shredders minus their vocalist.

Orpheus felt the ground disappear underneath him as the ghoul slowly slid him up the elevator wall. The pain was immense; Orpheus's eyes began to blur and roll back into his skull. He had to think fast, had to do something. Orpheus reached for his only hope — the Lyre-Axe and snapped it on.

The faceplate glowed, and it let out a deep feedback hum. Struggling to find its strings, Orpheus cranked out the roughest, rawest chord he could. Instantly, the air around him warped and distorted, and the EBN ghoul let him go and backed away. Orpheus grabbed the Lyre-Axe's whammy bar and strained the power chord for all it was worth, simultaneously holding the instrument like a weapon and shield.

The big ghoul released a pained, *"Waaagghhhhhhhggg!"* sound and backed up. Orpheus saw him off with the Lyre-Axe until he stepped out of the elevator. The door slammed shut. Orpheus found the control panel, smashed the up button, and felt it ascend.

He slumped against the cold metallic wall, gasping for air.

Axel had said he'd need a special deck to shred it down here. The Lyre-Axe had got him out of trouble, but he'd need everything possible to wrangle this nightmarish urban netherworld. The elevator opened, and Orpheus could see the roller shutter opening he came through beyond the veil of blue mist. Immediately, he shot out on his deck toward the shutter, ducked low, shot under it, and skated into the night.

Above him, the EBN camera caught all of this, and the Video Vampire, EBN's *numero uno* producer, had witnessed the entire incident.

So good old Orpheus wanted a one-way trip to hell, did he? The Video Vampire thought. Let's see if we can make that dream come true...

20

Orpheus rode back home to his container in the Grey Zone. He locked himself inside, back into the solitude and isolation he called a life. If it wasn't for his aching throat, his entire experience in that underground parking lot could have been written off as a bad dream from one of his depressed slumbers.

He tossed the Lyre-Axe on his bed, slumped beside it, and tried to clear his throat. It felt as raw and ravaged as if sandpaper had attacked it. Orpheus reached to the sideboard, grabbed a beer — plain white wrapper, simple black font reading *"BEER"* 100% Grey Zone approved — popped it open and sprawled out. The plain-wrapped piss made the pain go away.

Reaching out, Orpheus turned the dial on his old black-and-white tube set, and *Praise The Ray* settled on the screen through a slight fuzz of atmospherics. The EBN logo — the giant neon eye — buzzed on screen as it cut back from commercial. Orpheus remembered the giant eye in real life above the *Praise The Ray* soundstage; it was purple in real life. Orpheus snorted at the pointless memory, then shot up on the bed, tight and tense. The EBN bumper had cut to *Praise The Ray*, and what he watched on screen made his head pulse as if it would explode.

Hades was dancing to mundane Muzak, spinning and twirling a girl. Not just any girl, though, not one of their ghouls from a meat locker or that grinning Persephone Hecata. Eurydice was holding his hands and waltzing around the *Praise The Ray* set.

Orpheus shook his head and grimaced. Was he seeing things? Had he finally gone out of his gourd?

* * *

Behind the scenes of *Praise The Ray*, the Video Vampire and Persephone watched the show's live feed.

"There is something seriously lacking here, don't you think?" Persephone asked the Video Vampire.

"Uh-huh," was all he could respond.

"We're just not getting the performance we need from this woman."

"Uh-huh," the Video Vampire agreed again.

On-screen, Eurydice swayed lifelessly in Hades' arms as if she were a puppet with cut strings, and he was propping her up. Even for the void-oid, brain-dead crowd of *Praise The Ray*, she was too limp and lifeless.

"I think we have to get that musician back." Persephone nodded.

The Video Vampire growled, "Uh-huh."

"There's got to be a way," Persephone pondered out loud.

This was just the inroad the Video Vampire needed. He had something special for Orpheus. All he needed was the green light from Persephone. Now, it had come. He'd heard all the talk from Orpheus's friends about having a special board to shred the underground parking lot, in order to get to the heart of the EBN building, and it was all true. He'd watched them all talking outside the roller shutter doors on a hidden EBN camera. It was time to interject to make the prophecy come true. Orpheus had been nothing but a thorn in the Video Vampire's side. Now it was time to pull the thorn free and draw some blood that wasn't his own.

The Video Vampire reached under his desk and pulled out a jet-black-hell-deck. It was slick and stylish with an odd, otherworldly feel, like touching something inanimate that had become possessed with a dark, slimy spirit. He blew a layer of dust away from the board. Had it been that long since anyone had tried to shred their way down here? He grinned, remembering the last schmo that had tried to shred the EBN garage, and wiped away the dried specks of blood from its paint.

Persephone's face began to curl into a vile smile. It sealed the deal. It was time to send the deck out to find *Praise The Ray*'s new special guest star.

* * *

Orpheus was in shock. There she was, his wife, his true love, forced to perform like one of their un-dead ghouls. But the foul thing about it was even through the bad reception of his black-and-white set, he could see she *hadn't* been turned into one of their pale-faced drones. No, they had kept her in the same condition as the day they'd kidnapped her. She was perfect. Beautiful. They'd left her this way on purpose. To taunt and tease him, as if they knew he'd be tuned in at that second and there was nothing he could do. There had never been anything he could do. EBN pulled the strings, and his wife was the unwilling marionette.

Orpheus's hands squeezed into fists. Hades looked into the camera and winked with a sly smile.

Orpheus went berserk, trashing his container. Posters were ripped from walls; tapes and idiosyncratic knickknacks flew and smashed. Orpheus roared with rage until he was exhausted and collapsed on the bed. When he gave the screen his attention, Hades clapped as Eurydice was dragged limply away by two ghouls.

"What a performance," Hades said.

Orpheus stared at him with rage-filled eyes.

One way or another, he would give these bastards a performance they would never forget.

21

Back in his office, Linus worked to grease another slimy deal. "Man, hey man, Fred, come on!" Linus barked into the phone. "We're talking someone with major marquee value. This guy is a cult legend around here. Bus them in from suburbia, man. Fred, don't think small. We're gonna get kiss, kiss, kiss coverage! Print, radio, television. Let's go for the tri-state area!"

Fred, the manager of the Razzledome, wasn't taking it.

"All right, Fred... let's not let a few percentage points get in the way, okay? I mean, Fred, we both got overheads, right?"

Linus's assistant burst through his door, waving her hands to get his attention. A flush of anger painted Linus's face.

"Hold on a second." Linus clicked the line to mute it and barked, "What is it?" to his assistant.

"It's the production manager from that dance company on the other line. Orpheus hasn't shown up for rehearsal yet, and they've been waiting outside the Showbox for over an hour."

Linus's expression dropped like it would slide off

his face. "They're really pissed and want to talk to you."

Linus clicked his neck, wiped his brow, and lit a cigarette. "Shit. Tell them I'm right over there." Linus clicked the phone and made the line live. "Fred, look, I got a little forest fire here. Let me call you back, okay?"

Linus slammed down the receiver, picked up the phone again, and connected to the caller waiting — the dance company at the Showbox. He immediately went into full slime mode. "Hello, yeah, yeah. I — I — I know. I'm — I'm sorry about that. Look, I know he's a little moody—"

The voice at the other end raged, and Linus didn't blame them.

"All right. But his stuff is perfect for your show. Just give me a half hour to get him
there, okay? All right, bye. I'm out!"

Linus slammed down the line for good this time. He ground his teeth together and dubbed the barely smoked butt into an ashtray.

"Orpheus," was all he could growl.

* * *

Linus stood by a burning barrel outside Orpheus's container and banged on the door, shouting, "Orpheus!"

"Screw off!" came from inside.

"No way, *babe*." Linus pulled open the container door and went inside. Orpheus was zonked out on his bed, lying amongst the debris of his freak-out.

"I can see you've been doing some redecorating," Linus said dryly.

"Yeah," was all Orpheus could manage.

"You're an absolute mess. When are you going to

stop living in the past, my friend. You've got to move on."

"Where do you want me to go?"

"First to rehearsal," Linus snorted. "I'm tired of covering for your ass. I treat you like a brother — and all I get in return is bullshit."

Linus walked to Orpheus's bed and sat next to him.

Orpheus rolled towards Linus and stared at him with sad, dreary eyes. "It's all bullshit to me, man. I don't know who I am."

Linus sighed. "Then get some help. Look, there's an oracle coming in on the next tangent shipment tomorrow evening. Counseling, channeling, neuro-linguistic programming, video tarot — she's hot. See her."

Orpheus stared at the container's cold metal ceiling. "Maybe."

"Do it." Linus demanded. He grabbed Orpheus and dragged him to his feet. "Let's go."

Linus frog-marched Orpheus to the Showbox and made him meet-and-greet the dance company. Orpheus's body was switched on auto as he nodded along with everything Linus babbled; his mind switched off. He was as much an undead puppet as anything at EBN. Orpheus smiled vaguely and agreed whenever it was socially acceptable, though with no genuine feeling. While he faked interest with everything Linus wanted him to, one thing lingered in his haunted mind: the ghost of Eurydice's face.

22

A new container shipped into the Grey Zone: Open neon hands exposing their palms were painted on the doors, with a single glaring eye at their center. The container thudded down, and Orpheus walked over. There was a smell of incense in the air. Orpheus knocked on the door. After a moment, the oracle opened up.

The Oracle was dressed in majestic green and gold, with punk vibes. A new age mystic with a razor blade edge. She was attractive but stern-faced.

"Yes? What is your name?" the Oracle asked.

"O — Orpheus."

"Orpheus? The mortal who has gone where no man has gone before?"

Surviving *Praise The Ray* would be his legacy. Orpheus shrugged.

"What is it I can do for you?" she asked him.

"I want to go back to the underworld. That place, EBN. I know what it is now. It's not just a station, it's Hell."

"So?" The Oracle shrugged.

"So, you can tell me what I need to do, right? To find Eurydice?" Orpheus pleaded.

"Oh, I doubt that," the Oracle said with a quick raise of her eyebrows. "What you did was a one-shot deal. Besides, what do you think I am? The 911 Love Rescue Mechanic?"

Orpheus rubbed a hand over his face and stared at the Oracle.

"I'm in the forecast business," the Oracle said bluntly.

"Then give me a forecast," Orpheus said.

* * *

Inside her dimly lit container, Orpheus and the Oracle sat across from one, a cathode ray tube between them, pointing toward the ceiling.

"Place your hands on the screen," the Oracle said.

Orpheus did what she asked and closed his eyes. An electric charge fired through his flesh from the warm tube, and he yanked his hands away. Hades and Eurydice appeared on the screen, dancing between the flickers of a warped horizontal hold. The screen zoomed into Eurydice; she stared straight out at Orpheus, and then her image evaporated into a sea of static.

Tears welled in Orpheus's eyes, and a shiver rippled through his body. Then the screen crackled with bad reception; three electronic tarot cards appeared one after the other, and a synthetic electronic voice introduced each as they appeared.

"The Lovers."

"The Tower."

"The Hanged Man."

The Oracle inspected the cards and nodded. They all made sense in some otherworldly esoteric way.

"Don't force the issue," the Oracle said, nodding. "The price is too high. You can't live your life in a rearview mirror. You're lucky you made it back the first time from the studio. Whatever the relationship was, it's over. Move on... live your life."

"Life? I don't have a life unless I get her back. I don't have a choice."

"Listen, Boo-Boo," snapped the Oracle. "You'll join the pantheon of dead skate rock guitar heroes, but that's your choice. You're not ready to go back there."

"Just tell me where, how... whatever it is I need to do."

The Oracle glanced at the video monitor, studied the images on the cards, and concentrated. The couple embraced, the tall, dark tower, the silhouette of a hanged man. There was a distinct vision of a fate for Orpheus there — not the one he wanted. But a fate nonetheless.

Then a dead white point of light — maybe a burn-in on the screen, maybe a glimmer of hope — caught the Oracle's eye.

"Okay, you might get what you want. But it won't be what you expect."

The Oracle grinned at Orpheus. With the light from the cathode tube beneath her, The Oracle looked ghoulishly like a kid on Halloween with a flashlight under their chin.

"It's like this," she explained. "Go to the river. Wait for the heat to rise from the street. There is a shipping yard. number Twenty-Seven. Your destiny will reveal itself. If you're going to go there, go now."

The three cards shimmered to black on the screen.

"That's all I can tell you."

Orpheus nodded. He didn't have much to go on to find Eurydice, and the Oracle's words could be less than nothing, but he had to try.

"Shipping yard Twenty-Seven," Orpheus said with a nod. "Thank you." He ran out of the Oracle's container.

"Hey! That'll be fifty bucks!" The Oracle yelled after him.

23

23

Orpheus walked along the docks; plumes of breath visible in the cold night air. A rational part of his mind told him he was nuts, visiting a video oracle for advice on finding Eurydice. But he couldn't deny anything he'd experienced.

His time behind the scenes at the *Praise The Ray* studio, along with his descent into that mysterious underground parking lot, had solidified one thing: that place *was* Hell — literally. And Hades and Persephone were its king and queen.

He reached the shipping yard, found dock number Twenty-Seven, and looked around. Everything was locked up tight, dark, and gloomy. Orpheus wandered down to a group of transient punks fishing in water as black as the night above them. A shiver ran up his back like somebody had walked over his spine. He turned and looked around at the horizon towards an asphalt parking lot. Somehow, heat waves rippled there, illuminated by the neon glow of the Grey Zone behind.

What the—? There was a rubbery ripping sound, and a spray of smoke erupted from the edge of the parking lot. An acrid sulfurous smell hit Orpheus's senses. Then came a cracking sound as the asphalt gave way, and something shot up out of the smoke. It rose in the air so high it was silhouetted by the fat full moon. Instantly, Orpheus recognized the shape; it was a glossy black, gnarly, radical deck like no deck he'd seen before. It hit the ground with a clatter and shot towards him — jet-propelled, smoke pouring, and flames flaring from its back wheels. Then it came blazing towards him.

The Oracle and Axel had been right.

You don't find it. It finds you.

Holy fuck.

Orpheus walked away from the transient punks towards the board. It skidded to a halt in front of him. With trepidation, Orpheus picked the board up. It was hot; not untouchably hot, but heat rippled through its jet-black lacquer like a pulse. Orpheus flipped it over to reveal an alchemical logo with the grinning face of death at its center.

After studying the deck, he tossed it to the ground. As if by some autonomous intelligence, the board twisted in the air and righted itself, landing on all four wheels.

"*Wicked*," Orpheus whispered. He took out a pair

of fingerless gloves, gulped a lungful of air, and jumped on the board. Instantly, it took off.

Orpheus had no idea if he was shredding with the board or if the board was shredding with him. He tore along at top speed, kicking at the floor that moved fast beneath him. He had control of the board, could angle it left or right, and headed straight toward the shipping containers of the Grey Zone. Everything shot past like it had been filmed and played back at on fast-forward. Punks, metal heads, and zip heads peeled past him, becoming nothing but blurs. Shipping containers became blocks of bleeding color; other boarders out on their decks were knocked aside as Orpheus blasted through the Zone.

He flew down to the old access pipes that led under the Zone and, with the board's g-force, easily shredded a full 360 around the long, endless tubes. Flames erupted from the deck's wheels, illuminating the darkness behind as he burst out of the pipework into the night. He kick-turned the deck and spun it like a drill bit on the street's concrete, sparks grinding from the back of the board, and then he was off again.

He felt no sickness moving so fast. When skating with it, the board was part of him, and he was part of the board. There was a symbiotic relationship between the deck and the rider. Orpheus shot to the ramshackle skate park in the Grey Zone and hit the shipping pallet ramp so hard he took off thirty feet in the air. He grabbed the end of the deck, keeping his balance for when he hit the ground, but the deck absorbed the full shock, and Orpheus felt nothing.

Weaving the board back into the Zone, Orpheus understood the deck was a gift to get even, to find Eurydice.

He could use the deck in that underground EBN garage and shred his way straight to Hell.

24

Razoreus skated through the food vending section of the Grey Zone, where the air was thick with the scene of deep-fried delicacies of every culture. He was hungry, but as usual, there was no cash to rustle in his pockets, only jingle. He ground his board to a stop next to a phone booth and eyed the container with the pink neon sign: Zone Pizza. It was time to use the old okey-doke and dine Italian.

Razoreus slid through the booth's creaking door. The inside was coated in old spray paint and smelt like older piss. He grabbed the receiver, dropped a quarter in the slot, and phoned Zone Pizza. He watched across the street as the guy behind the counter answered the phone.

"Hey," Razoreus said, faking a voice that sounded more like Scratch. "I'd like to order a pizza to go. Make it for Willy Johnson. Pepperoni, olives, and mushrooms."

"Anything else?" the pizza guy asked.

"Nah, man. I'll pick it up in ten minutes."

Razoreus hung up and watched the pizza guy go to work.

Forty minutes later, around the back of Zone

Pizza, Razoreus hid in shadow, watched the pizza guy slam out of the container's back door, muttering, "Fucking time wasters!" He tossed a boxed pizza into a dumpster and stomped back in.

"Bingo." Razoreus laughed and skated to the dumpster. Inside, there were old greasy pizza boxes, empty soda cans, rotten food, shit scraped from their cookers. On top of the pile sat an upside-down box with the name Willy Johnson scrawled across the lid. Razoreus reached over, plucked it free from the pizza debris, turned it right side up, and opened the lid. The cheese and toppings were a stringy mess, all clinging to the pizza box's roof.

"Perfection," Razoreus laughed. He closed the box tight, slid it under his arm and skated off into the night.

* * *

Razoreus skated back through the Zone and went to Orpheus's container, the pizza still warmish under his arm. He arrived at Orpheus's door and banged twice. It was open, so he let himself in. Orpheus was inside, changing his T-shirt and wiping sweat from his brow, an intense look in his eyes.

"Hey, what's up?" Razoreus asked, looking around Orpheus's container. The whole place was a trashed mess. "What happened to your place?"

"Just doing a little remodeling," Orpheus said.

"You are weird!" Razoreus declared, then sat next to Orpheus on the bed. He noticed the jet-black-hell-deck that found Orpheus and instantly grabbed it. "Hey, this deck looks pretty rad. Where did you find it?"

Orpheus grabbed it back. "Don't touch it," he said. "I didn't find *it*. *It* found me."

Razoreus placed the free pizza between them. "Well, hey, you hungry? Check out what I scored dumpster diving." Razoreus yanked open the pizza box's lid to reveal the mangled, cheesy mess. "Pepperoni, olives, and mushrooms."

Orpheus slipped his leather jacket on and zipped it up. "I gotta go."

"Oh, come on," Razoreus huffed, "Let's do lunch!"

Orpheus laughed, "Okay, 'let's do lunch.'" He reached it to peel off a cheesy slice.

Razoreus pulled off a stingy triangle and stuffed a mouthful down his throat.

"Where are you going?' he asked.

Orpheus only chewed and ignored the question.

"Where *are you* going?" Razoreus asked again.

Orpheus said nothing.

"You're going to try that garage, aren't you?"

Orpheus sighed at his friend. "Let's just say I got a new deck, and yeah, I'm gonna try *that* garage."

"Try it, my ass!" Razoreus snorted. "How many times have Axel and Scratch warned you not—?"

Orpheus interrupted. "I know what they said." He took a breath and considered his reply. "It's dicey."

"Dicey?" Razoreus replied, wrinkling his nose. "That garage sounds like a meat grinder to me."

"Look, I've got the deck." Orpheus held up the jet-black-hell-deck. "I've got a chance. I've got to take it."

Razoreus shook his head. "That's totally mental."

"True," was all Orpheus could reply.

Razoreus shrugged. "Well, don't blow it, okay?"

Orpheus laughed again. "Okay." The two slapped palms.

"Why don't you stay around and crash. I'll be back in a couple of hours." Orpheus got up, grabbed the Lyre-Axe, strung it around his shoulder, and walked out of the container, the jet-black-hell-deck in hand.

Razoreus lay back on Orpheus's bed and stared at the ridges in the roof. He didn't get Orpheus at times. In Razoreus's mind, the guy had it all, he was a kick-ass rock and roller with a following, and Eurydice was long gone.

"Mental," was all Razoreus said to himself.

Then he remembered the way he'd felt at Orpheus's wedding, wondering if one day he'd have what Orpheus and Eurydice had. Suddenly, it all made sense.

25

Orpheus skated to the half-opened roller shutter door leading to the underground parking lot. He had no fear of entering this time — only resolve. The Lyre-Axe had warded off that big bastard EBN ghoul, and he had the instrument ready for action if he wanted to go for round two.

Orpheus kicked the jet-black-hell-deck towards the elevator, ground to a stop, and cautiously pressed the call button. The low, muffled rumble of grinding gears echoed; Orpheus, fearing the worst, backed up, bracing himself. He brought the hell deck up like a shield, his fingers on the Lyre-Axe's strings ready to use it as a weapon.

There was a rocking thud as the elevator stopped, and its doors creaked apart. Inside the elevator, the giant EBN ghoul glared down at Orpheus with a stare so evil it could pierce flesh. A huge toothy grin burst over his black lips as he noticed the deck and its al-chemical logo.

He nodded slightly, the deck somehow meeting his approval. "Right this way, sir," said the giant ghoul in a growling voice.

Orpheus slowly slinked into the elevator, back

against the far wall, keeping away from the oversized fiend. He'd heard rumors about this guy: Cerberus – the watchdog of Hades.

"Going up to go down, sir?" the big ghoul asked.

Orpheus just nodded.

With a push of a button, the big ghoul sent the elevator down. As the elevator descended past sub-level after sub-level, Orpheus swallowed hard, knowing he was entering EBN's underground domain. At minus sixteen the elevator chimed, and the doors shrieked open.

Outside was a small pool of light cast by a dim overhead bulb, highlighting a patch of cracked asphalt. There was nothing beyond but a black void. Orpheus stepped out. The big ghoul chuckled to himself, and the elevator door snapped shut.

A cold chill touched Orpheus, and he shivered. He stared into the void — nowhere else to go — then dropped the jet-black-hell-deck and thrashed into nothingness.

As he ventured into the gloom, everything around him began to eerily glow, and he understood. He was in some deep subterranean parking garage, and the concrete walls warped with wild psychedelic colors; bleached in a negative of red and orange and shot past in a surreal swirl as the deck picked up speed.

Orpheus veered the deck to a down ramp and plummet further into the garage's depths, spiraling around and around as a hellish heat grew hotter. He wiped his brow and kept his concentration as the special board blasted him faster and faster and straight down. The orange walls altered and shifted into hot pinks and purples; colors so vivid Orpheus had to squint to stop them from attacking his retina.

The deck's wheels rumbled beneath his feet. The terrain becoming rougher; and the garage's asphalt breaking up into shattered shards, pointed and jagged, like fangs in a vicious mouth.

The heat worsened with each level Orpheus; heat ripples danced across the ground. The pink and purple neon that engulfed everything curdled and turned a burning red and orange. A gust of awful heat blew over Orpheus's body. He winced but he kept his balance on the board.

Smoke began rising from the depths of the garage; the asphalt bubbled and burned under the deck's wheels. The entire parking garage was liquefying to molten slag, and ahead, the next down ramp had melted to a cut-off end. There was a deep drop into black nothing coming up fast. He couldn't trash inside here anymore; he had to get out, but he couldn't get off the deck, as it was the only thing keeping him from the smoldering ground. Then Orpheus found his chance to escape.

On the next floor was an old, blistered board propped up against the buckled railing of the parking garage. It led to an undulating endless sea of red and orange outside — a place that looked no deadlier than where he thrashed now.

Fuck it.

Orpheus aimed the board at the ramp, blew straight up it, and shot out into the fiery seas of hell. The board stayed beneath him as he fell and fell, deeper and deeper, down, down.

He hit the ground with an unbelievable crack; the deck absorbed the impact and pressed forward. Everything was burning; there was nothing but the curdling reds, oranges, and yellows of fire. Flames lapped over him and singed his hair and clothes. Orpheus looked down as he kicked the ground and felt an incredible heat rise through the sole of his sneaker.

Holy shit...

He was shredding the burning coals of Hell!

The heat was immense; he should be burning to a crisp, but the board protected him. Its black wheels churned up, spit sparks as it plowed forward. There was no way any mere mortal could shred this place on any average deck, but the board pushed him on. Orpheus screamed into the flames as he shot into the bowels of hell. Eurydice flashed through his mind: when they made love and kissed and held each other at night. This was his last chance, and the burning hellscape of the netherworld couldn't stop him.

He had to do this.

Had to find her.

"Eurydiceeeeeee!"

* * *

Eurydice, wearing a lurid, tacky dress, slouched through the door to her dressing room. She was tired from performing on the *Praise The Ray* stage. When she'd fallen off the roof of the parking lot on her wedding night, and an EBN ghoul had bagged her up and brought her back from the dead, she never thought she'd feel pain like her death again. After ten hours of dancing with Hades for a live TV audience of dummies, her feet told her otherwise. She slumped in a chair at her dressing table, staring at the blank screen of a monitor.

The door to the dressing room opened, and the Video Vampire popped his head around the jam. He held a grimy grin as he told Eurydice, "Five minutes."

Five minutes, then back to more banal dancing for the brain-dead masses.

"Now what?" Eurydice huffed. "Did they decide they needed an encore?"

"No." The Video Vampire slimily slipped into the room. "New routine." He held up a skimpy blue dress for her to perform in.

Eurydice closed her eyes at the dress and sighed, flinching as the Video Vampire moved closer to her and snapped on the monitor, showing her an image of a man skating through the flames of hell.

Eurydice drew a hard, long breath.

"Remember him?" the Video Vampire said with a hint of humor in his somber tone.

Eurydice didn't even feel the Video Vampire's clammy hands playing with her hair as she shifted forward to inspect the screen. EBN had tried to wipe her mind, as they did all their ghouls, but for some reason they could never quite completely rid the inside of Eurydice's head of her love for Orpheus. She had dreams and memories, moments when she knew there was more to life than being locked in a body bag inside one of EBN's meat freezers between forced appearances on screen. Eurydice stared at the screen and recognized the face that bellowed at the flames lapping all around it.

"Orpheus?"

The Video Vampire snarled.

"What's going on?" Eurydice asked, transfixed by the monitor.

"Looks like you and the old flame are getting back together again." The Video Vampire chuckled, a streak of nastiness bolting across his face. "He just won't burn out."

"You're not going to stop him coming here?" Eurydice asked dully.

"We tried," the Video Vampire replied, his hand more suggestive as it stroked Eurydice's hair. "He's too smart."

"Stop him," Eurydice snapped.

"Too late."

Eurydice slapped the Video Vampire's hand away from her.

"Stop him!" she shouted.

"Chill out!" the Video Vampire yelled back.

He turned to leave the room. "You're going to be Queen for the day in four and a half minutes." He slammed the door shut behind him.

Tears formed in Eurydice's eyes. The few scraps of Orpheus's memory that remained were now re-formed. A glimmer of hope twinkled again inside her. Maybe she could escape this televised nightmare and be in Orpheus's arms again.

* * *

Great balls of fire spat all around as Orpheus plowed through Hell's heat. He held up the Lyre-Axe, shielding himself from the furious flames.

The flames stopped and Orpheus found himself skating inside the sunken, dropped-off bottom stories of the parking garage he shredded when he'd left the elevator. Suddenly, there was a silence inside this sub-terranean place. All the warmth from the flames dissipated, replaced by an eerie chill. On one of the parking lot's nearest pillars was the spray-painted logo from the bottom of the jet-black-hell-deck.

He wasn't surprised the deck originated from here, but why did it help him navigate this under-ground highway to Hell? Orpheus turned and looked down the length of concrete pillars to their very end; a silhouetted figure walked out of the gloom of shad-ows, stopped.

And lit a cigarette.

Hades.

Orpheus flipped up the jet-black-hell-deck and

strode toward hell's head honcho. Hades then disappeared, dipping back into deeper shadows. Orpheus picked up speed. Rage ran through his veins. He had to get his hands on that bastard.

A huge plume of white smoke poured from behind a concrete pillar, and Orpheus stopped dead in his tracks.

"Well, Orpheus…"

Hades.

How could he appear there so fast?

Orpheus turned to the devious, devilish man.

"Welcome back," Hades grinned.

Orpheus said nothing.

"So, you wish to try for Eurydice again?" Hades asked, blowing smoke in Orpheus's face.

"That's right, Hades," Orpheus growled.

Hades took a huge drag from his cigarette and coolly said, "Okay, Orpheus, then let's begin."

Hades smiled a wicked grin at Orpheus. He could see terror and anger in Orpheus's eyes and loved every minute.

It was time for his final trick.

"Come, Orpheus. It's time for a new game," Hades said in his gameshow host voice. "It's time for *The Eurydice Door Show*!"

26

Back in Orpheus's container, Razoreus was laid out on his bed, the pizza box beside him was empty. Suddenly, his sleepy eyes popped open, disoriented as to where he was. Then he remembered: Orpheus had gone back to that weird ass-parking garage.

What was the time? How long had he been asleep and Orpheus gone? Razoreus wiped his eyes, looked around the wrecked container, then reached over and clicked Orpheus's tube set on. It was already tuned to EBN, and their glowing eye logo radiated from the screen. Overlaid on top of it were the words:

Special Report

An announcer spoke:

"We interrupt our regularly scheduled program to bring you this special EBN report. We go now live to The Eurydice Door Show, *already in progress."*

On-screen, Hades dragged Orpheus towards a makeshift stage at the parking garage's far corner.

"Oh, shit," Razoreus uttered.

Hades stopped and pulled Orpheus close. "Here is the deal," he said with an evil grin. "Persephone is standing in front of two sliding doors."

Orpheus turned to Persephone, now a demonic

hostess: her red hair big and wild, her eyes fixed forward blankly, her grin wide and toothy.

Hades exclaimed, "We have door number one…"

Persephone exaggerated her moments as she pointed to a roller shutter door covered in sprayed neon with a red dripping "ONE" at its center.

"…and we have door number two."

Persephone posed at the roller shutter door marked with a red dripping "TWO."

Hades went on. "Behind one of these doors in Eurydice; behind the other door… is your death."

Orpheus looked at the two roller shutter doors and clenched his teeth. Out of the corner of his eyes, he noticed the EBN production crew gathering; white-faced ghouls with cameras and a boom mic. Behind them, in the shadows of the parking garage, were a horde of white-faced ghouls from EBN's meat lockers, all unfrozen to attend this very special one-off edition of *The Eurydice Door Show*.

Orpheus swallowed and considered his options, knowing he was outnumbered in the Devil's den. He looked at Hades; his skin so tan now that it was almost red, and two tufts stuck out horn-like at his hairline. This far down in the bowels of the EBN building, Hades reverted to his real form, a creature with many names: Mephistopheles, The Prince of Darkness, Beelzebub, Apollyon, Lucifer, Diablo – the Devil. Yes, that's exactly who he was. And EBN was Broadcast Hell.

Hades laughed. "All you have to do is choose. Door number one or door number two. She's behind one of them."

He stepped forward to Orpheus face to face. "Do you still wish to play?"

Orpheus stared into Hades' eyes, determined.

"Yeah," Orpheus snapped.

* * *

"No!" Eurydice shouted at the monitor in her dressing room. She wasn't behind either door.

She threw herself against her locked dressing room door and pounded in despair. It was all a filthy setup. Tears poured down her face, her breath desperate and ragged.

Eurydice couldn't escape. It was pointless. She leaned against the wall and slid to the floor in sorrow. All she could do was gasp between her sobs, "I'm supposed to be behind the door."

* * *

"Okay, Orpheus," Hades hissed, "it's time to decide. Which will it be? Door number one or door number two? Door number one or door number two?'

Hades repeated Orpheus's choices over and over; Persephone maniacally pointed from door one to door two in rhythm. The crowd of white-faced ghouls all jeered and yelled their choices.

"One!"

"Two!"

"One!"

"Two!"

The slurry of noise only added to Orpheus's confusion. He looked from one door to the other, his heart aching at the choice. He had one chance to have Eurydice back. What door was she behind?

Hades grinned and chanted, Persephone pointed back and forth: *"Door number one! Door number two! Door number one! Door number two!"*

Orpheus gritted his teeth, took a deep breath, and yelled, "One!"

The crowd of white-faced ghouls all groaned.

"All right…" Hades said smoothly. "All right." He gestured to the crowd. "We have a decision! Door number one!"

Persephone's eyes grew big. She gestured and the roller shutter "*ONE*" began to rise.

Orpheus's stomach dropped.

The crowd of grey-faced ghouls cheered.

Backlit behind door number one were four odd figures: Hades' hell-spawn called the Furies, a grisly group he used for… the dirty work. Each had their long hair tied up, faces hidden behind grilled masks, and behind each mask were the eyes of a maniac, laughing, drooling madwomen. Each held a special weapon: a revving hedge trimmer, a shrieking circular saw, a roaring chainsaw, a swinging, blood-stained rope. They were four bloodthirsty lunatics, and the parking garage was their asylum.

Speechless, songless, Orpheus turned to Hades, who only shrugged and laughed in response.

The Furies rushed out, weapons brandished, ready for action.

Orpheus grabbed the Lyre-Axe and flipped it on.

Now we're ready to cook.

But as the frenzied Furies approached, the Lyre-Axe finally gave up the ghost. Orpheus coaxed out chords, but the Lyre-Axe rebelled. He tried to bend and warp the space around it, but all the instrument did was sputter. And die.

Orpheus never had a chance. The Furies grabbed him, manhandling him to a concrete pillar. The Lyre-Axe went flying and smashed to the ground.

The Rope Fury lashed Orpheus to the pillar, and the Saw Fury grabbed Orpheus's hair and yanked his head forward.

Orpheus grunted and yelled, he struggled to free himself, but it was too late. The Chainsaw Fury let it rip. Blue smoke poured from the saw's motor, the teeth on its chain spun to a blur, she brought the blade down on the back of Orpheus's neck. Blood, sinew, and bone sprayed as the Fury slowly — *slowly* — decapitated him.

Eurydice watched it all and writhed on the floor of her dressing room, a spasming mess of sorrow.

Razoreus jumped from Orpheus's bed, hurled his deck through the TV screen in an explosion of sparks. Tears fell from his eyes as he denied what he'd seen.

The four Furies stood drenched in Orpheus's blood. The singer's slumped body held to the pillar as his neck gushed red. With a final chew, the saw severed the last of the sinew. His dismembered dome cracked against the ground.

The Furies seized the head, each fighting to hold the gory prize. They tossed Orpheus's head between themselves; they danced with blood-frenzied joy as they played.

The crowd of grey-faced ghouls went wild for the macabre scene. Hades lit another cigarette and laughed. It was pure pandemonium, maximum madness. The EBN ratings would be through the roof!

Persephone wandered among the carnage, reveling in the revulsion of it all. She picked up the Lyre-Axe and studied the instrument. Orpheus's prized Gibsonian, as dead and useless as its owner. With a girlish snigger, she threw the Lyre-Axe to the ground.

As it smashed down, whatever crossed wire stopped it from working realigned, and the Lyre-Axe popped to life, letting out a long shrieking whine that warped everything in a twenty-foot radius.

Persephone and Hades went to scream, but the vibrations of the Lyre-Axe wiped them from existence; it did the same to the grey-faced ghouls and the Furies.

All that remained was a cold, eerie silence.

* * *

The door to Eurydice's dressing room creaked open, and the Video Vampire entered. He stared down at Eurydice's broken body on the floor. He yanked her up, brushed her hair from her face, seductively muttering, "You're on."

He pulled her from the room.

He had viewers to think about, and there was one final thing he had to do.

OVIDEO OBITUARY...

At last, the stones that heard
his song no more
fell crimson with
the Grey Zone poet's blood.

27

The parking garage in Hell was pitch black, but for a solitary spotlight focused on Orpheus's decapitated head.

Eurydice walked towards her husband with sadness set in her features. Tenderly, she took Orpheus's head in her hands and gazed into its glassy, dead eyes.

She whispered, "Orpheus, it's time to leave your body now." With the head, she crossed to a second spotlight, found her mark before Orpheus's headless body, tied still to the concrete pillar. She did her best to replace the head onto its bloody stump, to make him whole again. Eurydice took a step back to take him in.

Slowly, Orpheus's spirit emerged from the dead shell he once called a body — a naked, transparent version of his living self. Confused, he looked around into the blackness and then heard a familiar voice.

"Orpheus."

He walked towards it.

Eurydice was there with her arms held open for him.

Orpheus embraced her, and the pair held each other tight.

Finally, after all this time, they were together again.

Orpheus couldn't live without Eurydice, so now the pair would be together forever in death.

Hidden in the darkness, Hades and Persephone watched on.

"Well, well, what do ya know?" Hades said. "Together at last."

Eurydice and Orpheus parted, stared into each other's eyes, and then walked hand in hand to where the jet-black-hell-deck and the Lyre-Axe lay side by side. Orpheus bent down, picked up the Lyre-Axe, placed it on the deck, and pushed it out into hell's black depths.

It would go on to find a new owner now.

Just as it always did, they wouldn't have to find the deck.

The deck would find them.

From the darkness, the Video Vampire stepped into the corpse's spotlight and watched the reunited couple. He didn't like to lose. But now there was nothing he could do.

Orpheus's fight to find Eurydice had been good programming, it kept their viewers glued to the tube. But this story was over. It was time to let Eurydice out from under the black cloak of EBN and *Praise The Ray*, and let her move on to the afterlife.

They had kept her body and soul for entertainment purposes long enough. It was time to find new programming, get back to the drawing board. Eurydice was the Video Vampire's big break to move up the corporate ladder.

Still, Orpheus had to interfere and make himself a part of the show, ruining everything. He couldn't

143

David Irons

even take credit for Orpheus's involvement. Spitefully, the Video Vampire turned to Orpheus's corpse and yanked his head from his neck by the eye sockets.

It was a petulant piece of work, but he couldn't do anything else. Orpheus and Eurydice were free.

The EBN cameras broadcast across the wasteland of a world. Eurydice and Orpheus kissed, and as they did, their souls mingled in a glow of light, entwined forever as they passed over.

* * *

Depressed, Razoreus thrashed the streets on his deck. He headed down to the docks and stared out at the rippling blackness. His heart was heavy with grief, his head a scrambled mess of sorrow. He couldn't believe what he watched on EBN. Orpheus, his friend, the guy he looked up to most, decapitated on live TV. He wiped tears from his eyes; he felt alone and helpless. Then, out in the water, flames crackled upward.

What the—?

As he stared at the odd sight, he understood that something floating out in the drink was burning. He squinted and made sense of it — it was Orpheus's Lyre-Axe!

Then something else in the water caught his eye, something washed up, bobbing by the shoreline next to some graffitied rocks.

"Oh no," Razoreus uttered.

He rushed down to the rocky shoreline, ripped off his jacket, laid it wide and open on the ground, and reached into the water. Grabbing a hold of a handful of hair, Razoreus pulled out Orpheus's waterlogged decapitated head. He couldn't look at his friend's features; he wrapped the head in his jacket. Razoreus

144

stumbled backward and tried to climb up to Terra Firma, but stopped as an odd glow shimmered in the rocks beside him.

It was the jet-black-hell-deck Orpheus had in his room earlier that evening.

He remembered the conversation he had with Orpheus.

"Hey, this deck looks pretty rad. Where did you find it?"

"Don't touch it," Orpheus had replied, "I didn't find *it*. *It* found me." Now Razoreus had found it. Or had the deck found him?

An idea exploded in Razoreus's mind.

* * *

Razoreus thrashed down to the underground EBN parking lot Scratch and Axel had told him not to go to on the jet-black-hell-deck. He ducked down and boarded under the half-closed roller shutter. He skidded to the elevator door covered in spray-painted warnings and pressed the call button.

Razoreus swallowed and composed himself, his head filled with ideas of vengeance. The elevator door opened, and a giant ghoul leered down at him.

"Going up to go down, sir?" the big ghoul growled.

Razoreus backed up in shock as smoke poured from the ghoul's black lips.

"No way!" Razoreus exclaimed.

The big ghoul growled in some hellish language, anger twisting his awful face. He pulled out a portable tube TV set and pulled the trigger. A high-powered blast of condensed cathode rays burst out of the screen, forming the three-dimensional graphic of a purple eye logo sparking and crackling in the air.

Razoreus grabbed a pair of sunglasses from his pocket and plugged them into his face to protect his eyes from the hypnotizing cathode rays as they warmed his flesh. Razoreus jumped onto the jet-black-hell-deck to escape, but the signal from the cathode rays fried it, and black smoke plumed from the board.

"Hey! What's going on?" Razoreus bailed from the board.

The deck spun autonomously on the ground, then lifted, tumbling into the air, spinning straight into the ghoul's outstretched hand. The giant backed into the elevator, taking the board back to hell where it belonged.

Razoreus high-tailed it out of the parking garage, back onto the streets, and sped back to the Grey Zone, never looking back. He'd found the board; it hadn't found him.

This wasn't the way he was going to avenge Orpheus. Plan B.

28

After Razoreus left the Euthanasia garage, it was clear to the Zoners that there wasn't really anything they could do for Orpheus. He was gone. Axel, Scratch, and Razoreus figured the network would catch up with all of them sooner or later. But in the meantime, they all figured they could have a ripping rad time trashing the network signal. Axel called in a few favors from his fellow veterans of the Contra Drug Wars and got his hands on some holdovers from the battlefield.

It was a dream come true.

It was time to stop the masses from catching the wave. Time to end that fucking dish and prevent its signal from beaming into their smooth brains. Axel put together a tasty concoction of C-4 and other household items, attached a remote detonator, and with a little sneak work, the trio crept up on top of the huge monolithic glass EBN building to the satellite dish. The dish stared like a giant eye; it was time to make EBN go blind.

Razoreus and Scratch ran up to the dish, planted the C-4 at its base on the communication junction box, and then ran back to Axel, hiding behind a section of a ventilation shaft. Axel held the detonator in his hand, ready, a shit-eating grin on his face as he pressed the button.

It was the most glorious sight he'd ever seen; the most awesome sound he'd ever heard.

The dish cracked and splintered into shards as it blew across the rooftop. The orange explosion rocked the Grey Zone. The central hooked antenna fired off into the night. Fragments of the destroyed dish peppered over the trio's hiding place.

Axel, Scratch, and Razoreus all cheered and hugged seeing their hard work reduce the dish to a burnt-out stump. Razoreus and Scratch wheeled Axel back to an access vent and returned to the streets. They cheered, hollered, and whistled. Tonight, the airwaves were free of any microwave broadcasts from Hell.

That'll teach those EBN fucks.

* * *

Around a burning fire next to a half-pipe in the Grey Zone, Axel, Scratch, and Razoreus sat silently with some other boarders, watching the flames. Scratch took out two candles, lit them from the fire, and placed them on an old wooden crate. Then Scratch pulled something wrapped in an old torn denim jacket and placed it between the candles. It was Orpheus's bone-white skull. This was his Altar.

The boarders all held their heads in respect.

At first, it would bother Axel when they did these little rituals. Axel remembered that during the war he'd run across a tribe in the jungle that kept the skulls of their ancestors around to protect them in the belief that they would retain the wisdom of their forebears.

What the hell? Axel thought looking around at the Zoners. Anything that anchored a little meaning in their life couldn't hurt them.

Right now, these guys think Orpheus was cool because he played on a *PTR* show and skated the Euthanasia garage. Maybe someday they will understand why he did it.

For love.

For the future.

Razoreus placed a boombox on his lap, plugged in the cassette Orpheus gave him, and pressed play — Orpheus and the Shredders' music jammed out of the speakers.

This little ritual made Axel think of the time before the war.

A time when he was happy.

A woman.

She was beautiful.

Axel continued staring into the empty sockets of Orpheus's skull.

I hope you found the happiness in death that you wanted in life, my friend.

Scratch thumbed over their shoulder to the half-pipe. Razoreus and the other boarders picked up their decks and ran to its top. One by one, as Orpheus's music belted out into the night, the boarders all began to shred the half-pipe at full speed, twisting and flipping in the air, pushed on by the music to go faster and faster.

"That's it!" Axel yelled. "Shred it! Shred it!"

The boarders flew up the half-pipe higher and higher, almost disappearing into the night sky with the air they were getting.

"Go on! Yeah!" Axel bellowed.

The boarders became a blur, flashing up and down, illuminated by the fire burning before

Orpheus's skull. This was it. It was time to fight back.
The dish was the beginning. It was time to tear everything in this miserable fucking Grey Zone down.

Axel raised his arms in the air and screamed into
the night.

"Remember Orpheusssssssss!"

The Zoners thrashed, and the Grey Zone hummed
its percussive rhythm to entertain the gods who were
always watching.

A final Ovideo:

Its message scrolled out in blue for no one, for no one paid this one any more attention than they did any of the others, or than they would to any that would follow.

Still:

> Meanwhile the fleeting shade
> of Orpheus
> had descended under earth:
> remembering now
> those regions that he saw when there before,
> he sought Eurydice through fields fre-
>   quented
> by the blest;
> and when he found her, folded her
> in eager arms.
> Then lovingly they wandered side by side,
> or he would follow when she chose to lead,
> or at another time he walked in front,
> looking back, safely,
> at Eurydice.

Before the message could loop, a thrasher's brick shattered the glass-eye screen and blinded the video prophet.

...END TRANSMISSION.

The following pages feature images from the film *Shredder Orpheus* as well as behind-the-scenes photos. Used by permission.

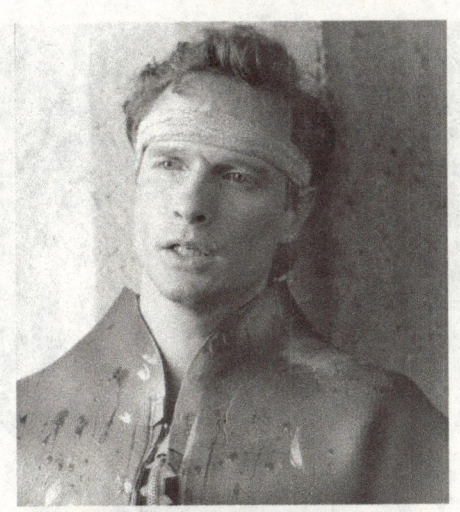

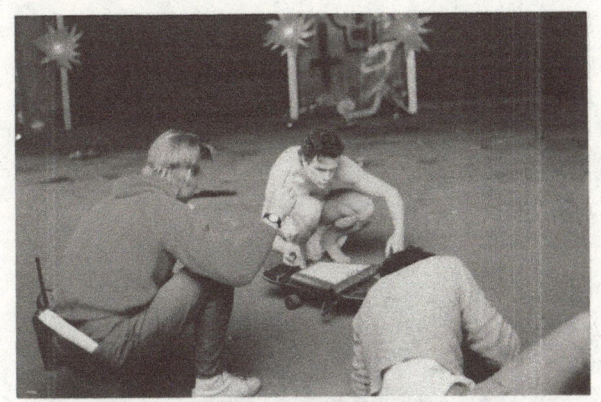

About the Author

 **David Irons** was the kid who went to his room to watch and read horror when his relatives came around. It paid off. When he left his room, he became an award-winning filmmaker and writer living on the south coast of England. His films, colorful and stylish in design, have won awards at the Cambridge Film Festival, Las Vegas VIFF Festival, and LA Independent Festival for cinematography, editing, writing, and directing. *7 Winters Alone* — a sci-fi, horror short — was a winner in David Lynch's 2014 Short Film Competition.

In 2019, David published his first novel, *Night Waves*, followed by *Night Creepers*, *Polybius*, and *The Bloody Tracks of Bigfoot* in 2020-2021 from Severed Press. Since then, David has become a Splatterpunk award-nominated writer for his '80s summer camp slasher, *Don't Go To Wheelchair Camp*.

The moral of this story is to be weird and stay in your room. It pays off in the end.

THE RETRO MASS MARKET COLLECTION

COLLECT THEM ALL!

- ☐ HELLRAISER: THE TOLL
- ☐ FRIGHT NIGHT
- ☐ RE-ANIMATOR
- ☐ HARDCORE
- ☐ WISHMASTER
- ☐ HELLRAISER: BLOODLINE
- ☐ TITAN FIND
- ☐ CREATURE
- ☐ VAMP
- ☐ SCARED TO DEATH OF UNKNOWN ORIGIN
- ☐ MANBORG
- ☐ ATTACK OF THE KILLER TOMATOES THE SPECIAL
- ☐ TAMARA
- ☐ FORBIDDEN ZONE
- ☐ COMMANDO NINJA
- ☐ LONG WEEKEND
- ☐ THE ODD JOB
- ☐ BLUE SUNSHINE
- ☐ THE BARN
- ☐ MOTORBOAT
- ☐ HOUSE SHARK
- ☐ HOUSE SQUATCH
- ☐ SHE KILLS
- ☐ AMITYVILLE DEATH TOILET
- ☐ SQUIRM
- ☐ PUPPET SHARK
- ☐ COCAINE SHARK
- ☐ CRUEL JAWS
- ☐ SPLICE
- ☐ ROBOT NINJA

- ☐ PLAN 9 FROM OUTER SPACE
- ☐ CIRCUS OF THE DEAD
- ☐ NIGHT OF THE DEMON
- ☐ MARDI GRAS MASSACRE
- ☐ LIFE CYCLE
- ☐ CHOPPING MALL
- ☐ ALL THROUGH THE HOUSE
- ☐ CHRISTMAS WITH THE DEAD
- ☐ FLESH EATERS
- ☐ VIRUS
- ☐ RATS: NIGHT OF TERROR
- ☐ CUBE*
- ☐ DEADGIRL
- ☐ SLEEPAWAY CAMP*
- ☑ SHREDDER ORPHEUS
- ☐ THE AMAZING BULK*
- ☐ THE RETURN OF THE AMAZING BULK*
- ☐ SWITCHBLADE SISTERS*
- ☐ THE DEAD NEXT DOOR*
- ☐ REDNECK ZOMBIES*
- ☐ SPIDER BABY*

*Coming Soon

www.ingramcontent.com/pod-product-compliance
Lightning Source LLC
Chambersburg PA
CBHW010932120626
46552CB00009B/3225

* 9 7 8 1 9 6 6 0 3 7 1 9 4 *